Blessed

ALSO BY SHERRY ROBINSON

My Secrets Cry Aloud

BLESSED

A NOVEL

Sherry Robinson

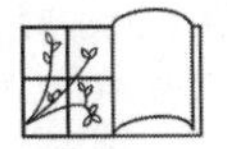

Shadelandhouse Modern Press
Lexington, Kentucky

A Shadelandhouse Modern Press book

Blessed, a novel

Published in the United States by:
Shadelandhouse Modern Press, LLC
Lexington, Kentucky
smpbooks.com

First edition 2019
Shadelandhouse, Shadelandhouse Modern Press, and the colophon are trademarks of Shadelandhouse Modern Press, LLC.

LCCN 2019937296
ISBN 978-1-945049-10-1
Printed and manufactured in the United States
Book design and page layout: Benjamin Jenkins
Cover design: Matt Tanner
Cover photo illustration: Shutterstock/Nithid
Production Editor: Stephanie Underwood

for Tiger Pennington
whose godly heart inspires me

BLESSED

Everyone in Mercy knew Reverend Grayson Armstrong, so it was no surprise that word of his sudden passing spread quickly. There were those who congregated at the Ignite Community Church to pray and weep, and those who gathered around Natalie and the children to mourn—and there were those who huddled in small groups at the beauty salon, the pool hall, or the grocery aisle to gossip. Whatever else may have been true, it was certain that there were few in the small town, except maybe for the very young, who had nothing at all to say about Grayson's passing.

But the truth was, the town had been talking about Grayson Armstrong ever since the dark-haired man drove into Mercy, Kentucky, twelve years before in his silver convertible with his pretty wife and two rambunctious boys. He had come to preach his trial sermon to a congregation that hadn't had a new pastor in twenty-three years. They asked him to come, sight unseen, and though they knew he was only twenty-eight, they were still surprised when he stepped out of the car beside the small red-brick church.

Fred Taylor was the first to see Grayson. He saw the shoulder-length hair and the ill-fitting suit. Don't look like any preacher I've ever seen, he thought. *He looks like a little boy.* His stomach tightened. People had counted on him, as the chairman of the search committee, to find a good replacement for Reverend Gillman. They wouldn't care how hard it had been to attract anyone, especially a well-seasoned preacher, to this dying town. They wouldn't believe that of the handful of applications the church received, this young man was the best of the lot. *There's going to be hell to pay*, he sighed, *especially when Reed gets a hold of this.*

He swallowed hard as he headed to the silver car, his hand outstretched, trying for all the world not to look worried.

"Reverend Armstrong?"

"Yes—and please, it's Grayson." The young man smiled, flashing a great number of his perfectly aligned teeth, and offered a firm handshake. "This is my wife, Natalie, and our boys, Tyler and Blake," he said as a slender blonde woman came around the car with a couple of towheaded boys trailing behind her.

"Pleased to meet you. Welcome to New Hope Baptist Church," Fred managed to say. He couldn't have imagined a future where Grayson would transform New Hope into Ignite, losing both denominational identity and congregants along the way.

"We're very excited to be here this morning, Mr. ..." Grayson said.

"Taylor. Fred Taylor. I'm the chair of the search committee."

"Of course. We spoke on the phone."

Grayson's warm smile should have made Fred more at ease, but instead he shifted his weight from one foot to the other. He wanted a cigarette, wanted a long draw to take the edge off this moment, but Effie had made him promise not to smoke in front of the visiting preacher. Now, looking at the long-haired young man, Fred wasn't sure it would have mattered. *Probably smoked a few himself,* he thought. *Maybe even worse.*

He was relieved when Tom Slater and Sandy Bell came up beside him. He watched as the choir director, whose gray hair had been in that same flat top as long as Fred could remember, and the organist, whose bleach-blonde curls were piled on top of her head, greeted the young family. Fred wondered if Grayson was a little too eager to make an impression, laughing as if every phrase uttered by Tom was very amusing. No matter, though, because Tom and Sandy seemed captivated.

Grayson was so absorbed in the introduction that he was

oblivious to Blake and Tyler, who had climbed on top of a retaining wall and were walking along it like a tightrope. Only Natalie's frantic "Boys!" and her dart in the direction of the wall drew Grayson's attention away from the others and, with a quick "excuse me," sent him to Natalie's side.

"Well aren't you adventurous little boys!" a bird-like voice said as Grayson lifted the squealing boys from the wall and set them on the sidewalk. He looked up, just as he whispered something in Tyler's ear, to see a gray-haired woman smiling down at the children as if they were cherubs.

"They do keep us running," he smiled back, answering for the boys.

"I'm Effie Taylor. Fred's wife," she said as Fred joined them. "It's such a pleasure to meet you Reverend Armstrong."

Fred would have marveled at the almost syrupy warmth in her voice if he had not known that her voice always carried the same sing-song lilt as if she was always talking to her school children. She gathered Natalie and the two boys like a sheep dog gathering a few wayward sheep. The children's programs were in the annex and she had come to help them find their way. Fred watched as Blake, who was four, skipped ahead of the ladies and Tyler, who at seven was too old for skipping, marched beside Effie. Fred admired Effie's ability to take charge in such a sweet and tender way. In forty-two years of marriage, he had learned to appreciate it, even depend on it.

Just before entering the building, Tyler turned to wave, flashing a smile that was every bit his daddy's. Grayson returned the wave with a wink and quick nod—a reminder of an agreement, Fred speculated. Once the children had disappeared through the annex door, Fred ushered Grayson into the sanctuary.

The inside of the church smelled of tradition. Dark walnut pews filled the room with an earthy heft that mingled with the mustiness of old hymnals and timeworn fabrics. The black walnut paneling pulled tight and snug around the room like a woolen coat on a frigid winter morning. Pale light from the six translucent windows along the sides of the sanctuary and a group of giggling teenage girls in the corner kept the room from feeling like a mausoleum.

Reed Hyden hurried down the aisle to greet Grayson and Fred at the back of the church. As chairman of the deacons and a long-time member, everyone would be looking to him for his reaction to the prospective preacher. Without realizing he had done so, Fred sucked in a breath and held it. But when Reed extended his hand and put a friendly hand on Grayson's shoulder, Fred blew a puff of relieved air. Other members of the congregation greeted the young preacher warmly. No one sent so much as even a short questioning glance in Fred's direction. *Maybe it won't be so bad after all*, he sighed.

A few minutes before eleven, Fred guided Grayson to the pulpit and the throne-like chair perched on it. Despite his lanky frame, Grayson looked like a child playing grown-up sitting in that chair. Fred wondered what this young man from a big city was thinking when he looked out over the half-filled pews or the choir, all ten of them, in their ivory robes and royal blue stoles. Meager as their numbers were, the congregation seemed eager to impress the new preacher. They sang the hymns with sincerity and read responsively with precision. The choir performed an inspiring song in three-part harmony. It was a magnificent prelude, they hoped, to the eagerly anticipated sermon.

When the choir sat down, Reed climbed the pulpit steps. He had volunteered to make the public introduction, which was a relief to Fred because, even to a small group, speaking on such occasions evoked red blotches on his neck and cheeks. He probably shouldn't have been concerned, he realized now. After all, how long was it going to take to describe this young man's brief experience? Reed handled the introduction with his usual charm, leading applause as he stepped back and made room for Grayson to stand. Rising from the chair, Grayson met the applause with an embarrassed smile and quick wave of his hand. He touched Reed's shoulder, nodded his appreciation, and then moved to his place behind the podium.

He laid his Bible, still unopened, on the podium and stepped out from behind it. Except for a couple of coughs and the creaking of pews as people shifted position, the room was quiet. A few people sent a bewildered look to their neighbor in the pew.

"Blessed," he finally said, letting the word hang in the air a moment before he continued. "What on earth does it mean to be happy, to be truly content? Are *you* happy?" Grayson's gaze landed on an elderly woman in the second row. She was startled and embarrassed by the attention. "Are you happy?" Grayson's gaze moved on to a gentleman on the other side of the aisle. As he scanned the room, his eyes reflected an affection for what he saw there. He looked—even if just for a moment—at every person. Most of them were older than him, much older actually.

"Without a doubt," he continued "to be offered such happiness, much less experience it, is often beyond our comprehension. But God desires it for us. He wants us to be blessed. In fact, this divine proclamation of favor, of perfect happiness, appears over three hundred times in the scripture. But before we get too excited or too complacent, we need to be aware the divine happiness that is offered—that is promised—in the scripture will be found in some of the least likely places.

"As Jesus began his ministry, people by the thousands flocked to him. Hurting people. Broken people. People who had been discarded. They pressed close, craving relief, yearning for happiness. And when he saw their need, when he saw their pain, he climbed a hillside and proclaimed that happiness was within their grasp."

Grayson again surveyed the room as he recited the scripture, but this time he lingered at each face, speaking the words as if they were an intimate and personal covenant.

"Jesus said to them,

BLESSED ARE THE POOR IN SPIRIT, FOR THEIRS IS THE KINGDOM OF HEAVEN.

BLESSED ARE THOSE WHO MOURN, FOR THEY WILL BE COMFORTED.

BLESSED ARE THE MEEK, FOR THEY WILL INHERIT THE EARTH.

BLESSED ARE THOSE WHO HUNGER AND THIRST FOR RIGHTEOUSNESS, FOR THEY WILL BE FILLED.

BLESSED ARE THE MERCIFUL, FOR THEY WILL BE SHOWN MERCY.

BLESSED ARE THE PURE IN HEART, FOR THEY WILL SEE GOD,

BLESSED ARE THE PEACEMAKERS, FOR THEY WILL BE CALLED THE SONS OF GOD.

BLESSED ARE THOSE WHO ARE PERSECUTED BECAUSE OF RIGHTEOUSNESS, FOR THEIRS IS THE KINGDOM OF HEAVEN.

BLESSED ARE YOU WHEN PEOPLE INSULT YOU, PERSECUTE YOU AND FALSELY SAY ALL KINDS OF EVIL AGAINST YOU BECAUSE OF ME."

Fred had unknowingly pressed his back against the pew, tensing his shoulders, as the service began. But as he listened to Grayson, the distractions faded from his mind. He was no longer aware of anyone else in the room, no longer vigilantly watching for accusing looks of disappointment. Instead, he felt the tightness in his body fall away. He was now only aware of the light that filtered through the colored-glass windows—casting brilliant white circles on the floor while orange halos of light danced nearby—and of the words that rushed from the pulpit in waves and then receded, gently, leaving something fresh, something new.

Something new *had* happened for Fred that morning. He had been reborn. But birth can be a difficult process. He could not have imagined on that day, or the day he called Grayson Armstrong and asked him to be their pastor, how difficult the process would be. In the years that followed it seemed as if no one in Mercy had been untouched by the young man who came to town pointing the way to blessedness. Now, in the face of an unthinkable reality, many of them were left to wonder how they would ever be comforted.

BLESSED ARE THOSE WHO HUNGER AND THIRST

RAMIE

PREACHERS AIN'T WORTH SHIT. Pardon my French, but that's what my daddy always said. As far as he was concerned, preachers are either hypocrites or they act "holier than thou." Daddy didn't have much use for them and frankly I don't usually either. So if I had known the first time I saw Grayson Armstrong that he was a preacher, I wouldn't have given him more than the time of day.

I was behind the counter getting the BLT for table four, so I didn't see Grayson come into the diner. When I turned around with the plate in my hand, all I saw was a couple of dark silhouettes in the door.

"Be right with you," I nodded in the general direction of the door on my way to table four.

"No hurry." The words carried the smile that must have been on the face of the man who said it—that seemed to always be on his face, come to think of it.

I set the BLT in front of Ed, who comes in every day for lunch.

"Thanks, Ramie. Be sure to check back with me later so we can talk about a little dessert." He winked, knowing I would catch his meaning. Like that was hard to do. He had that smarmy grin on his face that makes me want to throw up.

"I'll check back on you in a little bit, Ed." I gave him a weak smile so I wouldn't lose my tip, or my job. Melvin had already warned me that if he caught me being rude to another customer he'd fire my ass and not think twice about it.

By that time of day, I'd already been on my feet for over six hours, so I wasn't in the best of moods. I hated being on my feet all day. I hated that ugly yellow uniform that held the smell of grease no matter how many times I washed it. The truth is, I hated the diner, and I wouldn't have worked there if I didn't have to. Daddy taught me that it's not what your job is that matters. It's that you do an honest day's work. He was big on honesty. So I did my best to work hard and not complain. I swear to God, Daddy would have thought differently if he seen the way men like Ed look at me—like I'm on the menu. I've seen that look too many times. Don't matter if they're married or what side of the tracks they're from. Men just want one damn thing and they just assume I'm nothing but trailer trash so I'll give it to them.

I was still fuming about Ed when I took Grayson and the other man to the booth in the back corner. I shoved the menus in their hands without even really looking at them and headed back to the counter. One of them grunted his disapproval but I didn't care, even when Melvin glared at me. If he was going to fire me, he could just fire me. It's not like he was any different than any of the other men.

It wasn't until I was filling their water glasses that I took a good look at the men in the corner booth. Neither of them dressed like they'd come in from work, at least not from any of the nearby offices. I recognized the older man. Hank is a fixture around here—the town drunk. I can't tell you how many times I've caught him rummaging through our dumpster out back. That day, like always, Hank was wearing a T-shirt that was at least one size too big for him and it had some kind of stain on it. His jawline line was dotted with gray and black stubble that matched his salt and pepper hair, which was in need of a wash and a trim.

The other man was young and handsome. He wasn't scruffy

like Hank, but he had on an old T-shirt that was ripped at the neckline and had some grease markings on the front. I had a horrible feeling that not only was I not going to get my tip but also that there was a good chance I might also get stiffed on the ticket. I probably would have kicked them out if Melvin hadn't been in.

"Sorry about your wait," I said when I got back to their table. "You ready to order?"

"We were ready ten minutes ago," Hank said.

"It's okay, Hank," the other man said, putting his hand up to gently quiet Hank. "We're not in a hurry, are we?"

"No, I guess not."

The man smiled at me and it caught me off guard. It was such a pleasant smile, full of straight white teeth. If he was on the streets with Hank, I knew he hadn't been out there too long.

"Since I haven't been here before, what do you recommend?" the man asked.

"Another restaurant." The words flew out of my mouth before I could catch them. I glanced around to see Melvin glaring at me, but the man laughed.

"Since I'm already here, how about a cheeseburger and fries. Hank, what about you?"

"That sounds good, Reverend."

I'm sure the man noticed my startled expression.

"Now, Hank, I told you that it's just Grayson. I don't like fancy titles." He smiled, a bit embarrassed.

I studied on the man while they were eating lunch. He didn't look like any preacher I knew. A few of the local preachers came into the diner from time to time. They were usually in their suits, but sometimes it was just a shirt and tie. The truth is, they always seemed to me like they were actors, talking and behaving in a way that just wasn't natural. Reverend Gillman, from the church across the street, was a nice enough man, but when he came in he was all business. He liked to make a show of holiness by praying over his meal and reading his Bible. He asked me once if I went to church anywhere, and I lied and told him I went to one of those holy roller churches, only I didn't say it quite that way. I knew that would stop any invitation to his church, which I had no intention of ever going to.

So when I learned that Grayson was now the pastor of that same church, I found myself watching him. I was surprised that Hank was as lively as I'd ever seen him, telling story after story. Grayson listened with intention—nodding and laughing as Hank talked. Seems to me that when some preachers laugh, they do it because they know it's polite to do so. But Grayson's laugh was down from his belly, full and real.

It's a sound I'll have in my mind for a long time.

FRED

GRAYSON HADN'T BEEN HERE a month when he asked me about the homeless in the community. I had a vague notion that we had homeless people in Mercy. I mean, all towns have them. I just hadn't ever given it much thought, so I had to confess to Grayson that I had no idea.

A few weeks later, he called and asked me to go along with him to find one of the places the homeless gathered. He'd heard from someone where it was supposed to be. I'd be lying if I said I was comfortable about going, but somehow when Grayson asked me, I just couldn't say no. When we drove into the empty parking lot of a boarded-up factory, my body tensed, especially when we didn't see anyone. I thought for sure Grayson would leave and that would be that, but clearly I didn't know enough about him at that point. Instead, he climbed out of the car, grabbed a bag from the back seat, and headed toward a low window where a board was hanging loose. He didn't look back to see if I was following, which I wasn't. Instead, he stepped one foot on a stack of pallets to test their strength and then climbed on up and through the window.

A dirt devil swirled a few feet from the building, sending bits of trash scooting across the parking lot. Years ago, this building was the pride of Mercy—pumping out automotive parts. The people who worked there, my son included, made good money. But then the company left for some other town and left behind desperation. Many people had no choice but to leave as well, chasing the jobs that seemed to be everywhere but here. Too many buildings in Mercy were like that one, deserted and depressing. Though I didn't like seeing them, I hadn't thought much about what was happening *in* them. I realized that I was about to discover what was happening—at least in this one.

When I stepped out of the car, I glanced in the backseat,

hoping to find a baseball bat left behind by one of Grayson's boys. With nothing there but a couple of superhero figures, I picked up a rock, shoved it in my coat pocket, and headed to the window.

The pallet stack was wobbly, and I almost lost my balance. How had Grayson made it look so sturdy? I felt the rock in my pocket, for reassurance, took a deep breath, and pushed the board open enough to climb through the window.

The stale odor of urine, sweat, and whiskey hit me as soon as I stepped in—long before my eyes adjusted to the dim light in that empty, echoing space. I heard the low voices and made my way toward them. Grayson's face was the first to come into focus, and I was relieved. He and three men were sitting on some crates in a rough circle.

"Pull up a crate," one of them said.

"I was wondering what happened to you," Grayson said as I dragged a crate to the circle.

"Oh, you know me and my terrible sense of direction." I laughed, maybe a bit forced, hoping no one noticed.

"Fred, this is Billy, Hank, and Clarence. Guys, this is my friend Fred."

The way we all shook hands and greeted one another, you would have thought we were at a church business meeting.

"So, Hank, you said you served in the Army?" Grayson continued.

"Yeah, I was in Nam. I can tell you, this here is easy living compared to over there."

"Fred was in the service, too. Marines. Right, Fred?"

I shifted on my crate. "Yes, the Marines. I stayed stateside, though. Bum knee," I explained. "My friends came back with stories, though. Sounds like it was brutal."

"It was brutal all right. Nothing like coming home, though. No hero's welcome when us boys came back."

"That's what I've heard," Grayson said, which reminded me how young he really was.

"I couldn't keep a job when I came home," Hank continued.

"They messed with my head over there, and I couldn't shake it. I'd do okay when I first started a job but then something would happen and the next thing I knew I was right back in Nam and I was blessing someone out. A couple of times I took a swing at someone and the boss called the cops. Didn't matter that I served my country. They'd haul my ass off to jail. I'd stay a few days and when I was released, I'd find a new job. It just seemed like I couldn't get along with anybody, not even my wife. After a while, I just got to a point that I didn't want to be around anyone and the feeling was mutual."

"Must be lonely," Grayson said, almost as if he was talking to himself.

Hank laughed.

"Naw. I kinda like being in my own company. These guys aren't so bad either."

"Well, guys, I want you to know you have a place to come if you need something to eat or a dry, safe place to sleep every once in a while. The church will always be open to you."

I tried to see Grayson's face because I couldn't be sure if he was talking about our church. When I was sure he was, I knew that the homeless men were the least of my concerns and the rock in my pocket was not going to be nearly enough.

REED

The dust and gravel kicked up behind my truck as I drove down that old farm road to the Bennett's house. I wished it was just a social call, but it wasn't. I had to find out for myself if it was true.

I was about six the first time my mother took me out to the Bennett's place. She and Addie Bennett had met in the Women's Missionary Union at church and became fast friends. They were best friends until Mom passed away. Even though she was younger than Addie, Mom always looked after her. On her deathbed, Mom made me promise to look after Addie—and Ollie, too—after she was gone.

Addie and Ollie Bennett were a sight. Addie was a foot taller than Ollie and when she was younger she had bright orange hair, "like the sunset," Mom used to say. Ollie was plump and had jet-black hair. Addie used to laugh at the silliest things—the cat chasing a bird through the yard or a wind gust propelling her thin frame down the road. Mostly, though, she laughed at Ollie. Not in a mean-spirited way. She was Laurel to his Hardy, always getting him into a fine mess and then laughing her way out of it.

When I was a kid, I hated going to that house. There just wasn't anything for a boy to do when his mom made him stay in the stuffy kitchen and draw pictures while she and Addie talked about quilting or gardening or a hundred other topics that bored me to tears. About the only thing that made those trips bearable was Addie's cookies or jam cake that were washed down with a glass of cold milk. It's how Mom always bribed me to go.

Now I didn't want to go for a different reason.

When I stopped in the driveway, I saw the detached garage was leaning to one side and the door was missing. One stiff wind would take that thing down. I could hear what certainly would have been my mother's disappointment had she been there telling me I should have gone out there a long time ago to help Ollie fix it.

The porch was sagging so much that I wasn't sure it would bear any weight, so I headed around back instead. Besides, I knew better than to go to the front door. Addie always said the front door was for company, not for family. She would have had my hide for such an insult.

When I rounded the back corner of the house, I could see the door was open. Addie was singing "Victory in Jesus" to the top of her lungs, which brought back such sweet memories. She and Mom used to sing in the choir, Addie singing many a solo in her time. By now, though, her voice was suffering from a lack of practice, since Grayson had replaced the choir with a praise band.

I felt a little guilty coming to her like this, involving her in this mess. Through the screen door, I watched her, her back to me, as she smoothed the table cloth. Her hands were not as steady as they once were, making the cup and saucer rattle as she sat it on the table.

"Are you just going to stand there all day?" she asked without turning around.

"Sorry, Miss Addie." I stepped inside. Every time I came to visit as an adult I was struck by how much smaller the kitchen seemed than when I was a boy, yet nothing had changed. Nothing. From the avocado green appliances to the brown and yellow giant flowers papered on the wall, it was like stepping back in time.

"I didn't want to disturb your singing," I continued.

"That caterwauling?" she laughed.

"It was beautiful. I miss hearing it."

"Like a toothache, I'm sure." She laughed again and motioned for me to sit down. "Care for some tea?"

"You wouldn't happen to have a glass of cold milk? And maybe a slice of jam cake?"

She grinned and lifted the lid from a Tupperware container to show me the cake topped with my favorite caramel icing. "I made it as soon as you called to say you were coming out."

"You're an angel, Miss Addie."

She sliced a couple of pieces and laid them on the same china plates she'd used for years, and then she poured two glasses of milk.

"So where's Ollie this afternoon?" I asked after the first bite of cake.

"Oh, he's out tinkering in the garage."

"Funny, I didn't see him when I came in."

"He might have wandered over to Charlie's. He's always pestering that poor young man. Probably makes him regret moving in next door."

"I'm just glad you have neighbors way out here. I worry about you two."

"We're fine," she said patting my hand. "But I do appreciate that you worry after us, just like your dear mother used to." She sighed. "I sure do miss her."

"Me, too, Miss Addie. Me, too."

"So what brings you out here? I'm guessing it wasn't just for the cake."

She was always one for getting to the point.

"I do hate to involve you in this, but I figure you already are anyway. I haven't seen you in church for several weeks. I was wondering what's going on."

"I thought it might be that." She gathered the last bite of cake from her plate and popped it into her mouth. She paused so long after the bite that I wasn't sure if she was going to say anything more. "So did he send you?"

"Brother Armstrong? No, I came on my own."

"Oh." She paused again and squished a few crumbs together on her plate with a fork. "I suppose I'm more disappointed than surprised."

"What does that mean?"

"I guess I hoped we'd have been missed by now."

"You have been missed—by me."

"But apparently not by him." She looked down at her plate but not before I saw tears forming. I placed my hand on top of hers.

"I'm sorry, Miss Addie."

"It's not your fault, honey." She slid her hand free to brush away a tear. And then she looked at me. "I've been going to that church since I was twelve. Went there one night with my friend, Elizabeth, for a revival and got saved that very night. Ten of us did, and Brother Malloy baptized us all on the spot. I met Ollie in that church and we got married there. I met your mother there. It was my church, Reed. *My* church. Do you know what I mean?" I nodded because I knew exactly what she meant. "But it's not that way anymore."

"I know. A lot has changed in the six years since he's been here."

"Too much change for me and Ollie. No more choir or evening service. Not even prayer meeting on Wednesday nights."

"Is that why you and Ollie stopped coming?" I asked. I had already heard the story from Tom Slater, but I guess I needed to hear it from her.

"No, not really. Oh, we'd been thinking about it for a while, with all of the changes he's been making. Our minds weren't made up until right before the Fourth of July, though. I don't think you were there that Sunday, but Brother Armstrong made a point of saying in his sermon that the American flag didn't belong in a house of worship. Ollie and I just looked at each other. Ollie tried to talk to him after the service, very nicely mind you, to tell him that we had always displayed the flag for important days like the Fourth. We need to honor this country and everyone who's fought and died for it—Ollie's brother and your father included."

"I can't agree more. I certainly understand why it upset you."

"He wasn't even listening. He just said, 'We're going to try something different.' Can you believe that, Reed? Like paying respect to this country is somehow sinful." Tears welled up in her eyes again and she had to swallow hard. "I don't think I can ever go back there."

"Please don't say that, Miss Addie. You won't be a stranger in your own church if I can help it."

"Thank you, honey," she smiled. "Your mama and daddy would be proud of you. I know I am."

I hugged her tight. It was like I was hugging my own mother again. "I'll take care of it, Miss Addie." She squeezed me again and then sent me out the door with a chunk of jam cake and a smile.

As I was climbing into the cab of the truck, I saw the rusty old Chevy sitting behind the garage. I remember the day Ollie drove that Bel Air convertible, shiny red and fresh from the dealer, into our driveway. Dad and Ollie looked over every inch of it and talked of V8 engines and horsepower. Ollie included me, even though I was pretty young. "Look here, Reed. This is a carburetor." I absorbed every word, every sight. Seeing that car rusted and forgotten made me sad. I would have given my eye teeth for it. Uncle Billy and I could have fixed it up real nice. Nothing better than taking a beat-up, old car and giving dignity back to it. Such a shame to see something that meaningful to me be abandoned.

I shook my head. I was more determined than ever to do something about Grayson Armstrong.

RAMIE

THE DINER IS BASICALLY empty most afternoons in between the lunch and dinner shifts. Gwen usually takes off to run errands, leaving me with the handful of customers. I don't mind, though. Gives me time to catch my breath and watch people strolling up and down the street.

That afternoon, I had only two tables. The three ladies from the knitting club, who usually stopped by for pie the third Thursday of every month, and Grayson. Since his church was across the street from the diner, he developed a habit of coming by several afternoons a week for coffee and a quiet place—his mini retreats, he called them. As usual, his table was spread with papers and a whole stack of books.

I went into the back to get the silverware so I could wrap sets for the dinner rush. Melvin was in his office. I could hear him grunting and muttering to himself, so I stayed clear of him. He was not in a good mood. Joe, who was cleaning the grill, looked up and rolled his eyes, nodding toward Melvin's office. He didn't care for Melvin any more than I did.

I was dumping the silverware into a big bowl when I heard the door chime. I grabbed the bowl and headed for the front. When I got out there, I saw that Grayson now had company at his table—a tall man with graying hair. He looked familiar but I couldn't quite place him. I put the bowl on the counter, grabbed the coffee pot and a menu, and headed to the booth.

"I understand what you're saying, Reed," Grayson said. "But I have to do what I'm being led to do."

"It's not just *your* church," the man said as he waived me off. His voice had a hard edge.

I watched the table while I was wrapping silverware. I couldn't see Grayson's face, but I could see the other man. His face was tight. In fact, his whole body was tight. Several times he pointed a finger at Grayson. I wished I could see Grayson's face because his normally slack shoulders were rounded and tense. I had never seen him ruffled and I wondered if his face was any softer than his shoulders.

I went in the back to see if Joe needed anything and when I came back the man was gone. Grayson was bent back over his papers and for a moment I wondered if I dreamed the other man.

After refilling the ketchup bottles, I made my rounds with the coffee pot. The ladies were chatting about a new pattern for a baby blanket, but they stopped talking and waited for me to fill their cups—like somehow this pattern was top secret. I grinned as I walked away. Those biddies didn't need to be concerned about me.

Grayson was staring out the window when I got to his table, so he didn't notice me, even when I asked if he wanted a refill.

"Oh, sorry. I didn't see you," he said after I repeated myself.

"Yeah, I noticed." I poured the coffee and set the pot on the table behind me. "You were a million miles away."

"Only a few hundred yards, actually." He was quiet again and looked out the window. I figured he wanted to be left alone. "You don't go to church, do you?" he asked without turning back toward me.

"No." I hesitated. Grayson had never forced me on that topic, so I wasn't sure if he had just been setting me up for this moment.

"What do you think of church people?" he asked.

"Church people?"

"Yeah, you know, religious types."

"You having trouble with some church people?" I asked.

"Nothing like that," he smiled. "Well, maybe a little like that."

"To be quite honest," I said, "I don't have much use for them. Too judgmental if you ask me."

"Sounds like you have some experience with that."

"No more than you have, it would appear." We both smiled.

The truth was that I did have experience. More than anything I wanted to tell him what it really was. But I had never told anyone, and as much as I had grown to like Grayson, I couldn't tell even him.

I couldn't tell him how my mommy used to beat me within an inch of my life. How she took a belt to me sometimes until she drew blood. It was always worse when she would come home from those holy roller meetings. She couldn't seem to find an end to all of the evil I was guilty of. I wouldn't cry outright when she hit me—wouldn't give her the satisfaction, which made her beat me even harder.

Daddy would come home and find me whimpering in a heap on my bedroom floor. He scooped me up and held me until my shivering stopped. And then he'd lay me on my bed, cover me up, and go find mommy.

"What in God's name makes you do such a thing?" I could hear him say, his voice low and deliberate. Daddy didn't like to yell.

"Don't you use his name in vain in this house."

"What the hell happened to you, Nan? You didn't used to be like this."

"And stop that cursing, too. I won't have you and her bringing judgment down on this house. She's a devil child, John, and you know it."

"Well, if she wasn't here, I would have been long gone," he said. I could hear the back door slam and I pulled the covers tighter. It was only then that I would feel the tears come.

No, I didn't care for church people, except maybe Grayson. I looked at him, his blue eyes looking up at me and looking so much like my daddy. I felt the tears ready to come and I had to look away. Out the window, I saw the growing purplish-black clouds hanging in the western sky.

"You'd better watch out," I said. "There's a storm coming."

EFFIE

THEY LOOKED LIKE A couple of drowned rats standing there just inside my office door. Water dripped from their hair and clothes into a puddle at their feet. Grayson looked absolutely pitiful sliding his satchel to the floor. I had been the church secretary long enough to know that the satchel probably contained pages of sermon notes and as many books as he could carry. The bag looked as soaked as he was, so I could only imagine the fate of its contents.

The other man was unfamiliar to me. His gray and black hair seemed to be matted, though it was hard to tell because it was soaking wet. I suspected he was one of the homeless men Grayson had been working with down at the old factory. Fred told me stories of their time down there. When Grayson introduced the man as Hank, I recognized the name.

"We got caught in the storm," Grayson said.

"Yes, I can see that," I laughed. "I'll go see if I can find some towels and maybe even some dry clothes. In the meantime, there's a portable heater in the closet if you want to warm yourselves."

"Thanks, Effie. You're the best." He flashed that boyish grin that I'm sure had gotten him out of a tough spot more than once.

When I returned a few minutes later, I could hear them laughing before I even got to the room. They were crouched in front of the heater and joking about needing a rotisserie to dry evenly. I handed them the towels that I found by the baptistery.

"Clothes are on the way," I said. "I called Fred and he is bringing some of his."

"He doesn't have to do that," Grayson said. I could tell, though, that he was grateful.

"Yes, he does," I replied with a wink. "Besides, it's almost quitting time. He had to come get me anyway."

"Oh, wow. I didn't realize it was getting that late." He looked distressed, but I couldn't pursue it further with a stranger sitting there.

I worried about Grayson sometimes. He had such a big heart and I'd seen it bruised more than once. Church secretaries see and hear things. I've heard people say some pretty hateful things to him—and behind his back, they'd say even worse. Some complained that Grayson didn't care about anyone but himself. I can guess I can see why they might believe it. He did have strong ideas about the way certain things should be done. But nothing he ever did was out of spite, or for himself, really. Of course, that didn't mean everyone understood it that way. He often pretended like the comments didn't bother him, but I knew better.

I remember that summer, I think it was the Sunday before the Fourth of July, I came into the office after church to put away the visitor cards. Voices were coming from Grayson's office, which weren't loud or even angry, just tense.

"Don't you see that it's disrespectful to our country and our veterans," the man said. I recognized Ollie Bennett's voice.

"I understand. Really I do," Grayson said.

"But not enough to change your mind."

"Why don't we just try it this year? Maybe next year we can plan a special picnic on the church grounds instead of something during the service. It would still be honoring the country and the veterans."

"It's not the same thing and you know it. As a matter of fact, it seems like very little is the same around here anymore. I don't think you're going to be satisfied until you've changed everything we've ever loved about this church."

When he left, Ollie rushed by my desk without saying anything or even looking at me. And then Grayson appeared at the door. He didn't speak, but I saw his face. I wanted to comfort the pain I saw there.

"It's okay, Grayson."

"It's never okay when you hurt someone," he said. He didn't mean it as a rebuke, at least not for me.

That was the Grayson I knew. That was the man who sat drying himself in front of a heater while joking around with a man most people would try hard to avoid. Fred would have avoided Hank, and people like him, at one time, before he started helping Grayson at the old factory. The change in Fred was slow, but now I don't think he could see himself going back to the old ways. Grayson changed that for both of us. He preached more than once about people "playing church." Some people took this as an attack on the church and accused him of teaching against the Bible. But Fred and I understood what he meant. So it didn't surprise me at all when Fred showed up not only with clothes but with some hot sandwiches for everyone.

While we were eating, we were startled by a flash of light through the window.

"Looks like the storm is kicking back up," Grayson said. He looked at Hank sitting comfortably in slightly too small, but dry, sweat pants and T-shirt. "You don't need to be out in this. Why don't you stay here tonight?"

"At the church?" Hank seemed puzzled.

"Sure. I told you that you are always welcome. Besides, if a man can't find rest in God's house, I don't know where he can find it. Right, Fred?"

Fred nodded, and even though we all knew there would be consequences, we set up a cot in the choir room. With Hank settled in for the night and Grayson in his office trying to dry out his papers and books, Fred and I braced ourselves for the storm.

NATALIE

IT WAS AN OLD argument we had that night when he crawled into bed around ten. For the fourth night in a row he had worked straight through dinner and again I was left alone to take care of the boys and a newborn.

I pretended to be asleep when he came into the room. As much as I wanted to let him know just how angry I was, I was tired of begging him to give as much energy to his family as he gave to strangers. So I just let him get into bed. That didn't stop me from fuming when his breathing slowed into a gentle rhythm, and I thought he had dropped off to sleep without even trying to talk to me.

I rolled over hoping not to cry, but I didn't succeed. Maybe it was post-baby blues, but I seemed to be at the point of tears all the time. He must have heard me sniffle because he put his hand on my shoulder.

"Are you okay?" he whispered.

"I'm fine."

"I've been married to you long enough to know that usually means you're not." He squeezed my shoulder. "What's up?"

I rolled onto my back and stared at the ghostly shadows created by the alarm clocks on either side of the bed. I wondered what would be the point of re-tilling the same ground we'd worked over so many times before. But I knew that Grayson wouldn't let it drop—not if he thought I was angry.

"It's the same old thing, Grayse. The boys and I missed you again at dinner tonight. How many nights have we had to eat without you this month?"

"I don't know."

"The fact that you don't know should tell you something."

"I'm sorry, Nat."

"Being sorry isn't enough. Not anymore. Those boys are growing up without a father, and Hannah won't even know you. It's like you're a stranger to us."

"That's not fair. You all are my life."

"It needs to be more than just words. We need to see—*I* need to see—that we are just as important as your job."

"Natalie, you know that I love you more than life itself. But you also know that my job is not nine-to-five. I have to be available to do whatever God is leading me to do—and whenever he says to do it."

"I hate when you do that. How can I compete with God?"

"You know that's not how I meant it, but ministry requires sacrifice—for all of us. We knew from the beginning that it would be this way."

"That was before we had three children. It's just harder now." My anger had subsided but I still couldn't hold back the tears.

"I know," he said as he pulled me closer. "I take you for granted sometimes, and I'm sorry. I promise to be home more." It was a promise I knew he meant, but asking him to keep it was like asking a river to flow uphill. It was against his nature to walk away from someone in need physically or spiritually. Back when we were first married, when we were still idealistic dreamers, I committed to this path—not just because I believed in it but because I believed in him.

"So what did keep you away tonight?"

"I was with Hank. He is so lost, so trapped in his own pain. There was a moment tonight that I thought maybe he could see a way out, but it seemed to slip away. Sometimes I think God chose the wrong person to do this. I am so inadequate to the mission."

"You are more than adequate for any mission—and for me." I was always surprised when this confident man I knew had self-doubt. "I love you," I whispered into the dark.

He pulled me in tighter, as if by instinct he was searching for sustenance like a root searches for water. Ministry is grueling and I knew he needed me to be strong. I wondered if I was the one who was inadequate to the mission. As I listened to his breathing ease into a gentle snore and I felt his arms grow heavy, I knew not only that I *had* to be that strong but that I *wanted* to be.

HANK

I HAVE THE SAME dream over and over. Same old fucking nightmare. God I hate that dream.

I'm walking in the jungle with my pal Robbie. We were in the same platoon in Nam and had become fast friends. Both of us were small town boys, me from Kentucky and him from Tennessee. Neighbors, we used to say. We southern boys had to look out for each other, especially on patrol.

The jungle is so goddamn dense I can barely see Robbie ten feet in front of me. We're wading through the brush, heading toward God knows what. We freeze at the sound of something moving up ahead. The air is thick and humid and I can barely breathe. I can feel the sweat soaking my fatigues and I want to wipe it from my forehead, but I'm too frightened to move. I look at Robbie through the brush. He looks back and I know what he's thinking. It's very likely that one of us—maybe both—won't be walking out of that jungle. Instinct kicks in and I nod at him. He knows. We drop to our bellies just as the bullets whistle overhead. My heart is pounding so fast that it feels like the earth is moving below me. *Is Robbie all right*, I wonder. I can't hear anything except the gunfire crackling in front of us. I slide my rifle slowly—too slowly, I tell myself later—beside my body until I can get it set. I'm going to kill these bastards if it's the last thing I do. Just as I'm about to pull the trigger, Robbie comes charging toward me. His screams are inhuman and I want him to stop. I beg him to stop. But he keeps coming so I roll over to get out of his way just as he falls beside me. His eyes are fixed on me, permanently asking me why.

Sometimes in the dream he's shot by the enemy. Sometimes I pull the trigger myself just to get him to be quiet. Sometimes he is burning up with napalm. But always—always—I wake up screaming in a cold sweat.

That's the way it was that night in the church.

The room was dark and unfamiliar. As my eyes adjusted to find the faint light trying to break through the window or under the door, I sensed the strangeness of the place. Shadows of objects I didn't know surrounded me. Rather than my heart slowing to a normal beat, as it usually did after waking from the dream, it continued to race. There was an echo of the dream lingering in the room and I feared it.

At the sound of footsteps just outside the door, I instinctively reached for my rifle. My hand frantically searched for it on the cot and then on the floor, but it found nothing. I slid off the cot and crouched near the door, which opened just a crack.

"Hank? Are you okay?"

The voice was familiar but it didn't calm the uneasiness. I didn't move or make a sound.

"Hank, it's Grayson."

When the door opened wider, I lunged at the shadowy figure and we both tumbled to the floor. I tried to overpower him, but he was strong. He repeated my name over and over, calm but firm, as he gripped my arms.

"Hank. Hank. You're safe. You're safe, Hank."

His face, which was now visible from the hall light, came into focus.

"Rev?"

"Yes, Hank. It's me, Grayson."

I let go of him and he eased his grip.

"Are you okay? I heard you screaming," he said. The tenderness in his expression brought me fully into that space and that moment.

"Yeah. It was just a nightmare. I have them all the time."

"It must have been awful. That was a terrifying scream."

"It's the goddamn war, man. I can't seem to get it out of my brain."

"I don't guess anyone who's been in combat ever does."

He stood up and reached a hand down to me. He directed me to a couple of chairs where we sat quiet for a few seconds in the now dimly lit room. I guess he was sizing me up, trying to figure out what to say.

"I can't imagine what it must have been like," he finally said. "But I'm here to listen if you ever want to talk about it."

"Talking's never done any good," I replied. "There are just some images in my mind that no amount of talking will ever take away."

"Then how about praying?"

"No offense, Rev, but after the war, I have to agree with Nietzsche. God is dead."

He smiled, which took me by surprise.

"I'm a Barth man myself. I believe he said something like 'to clasp your hands in prayer is the beginning of an uprising against the disorder of this world.'"

I grinned. "Maybe someday, preacher," I replied. But I couldn't see that happening and I think he knew it, too.

"Well, if it's okay with you, I'll pray for the uprising for you."

I nodded, not that I was convinced it would do any good. In fact, I was pretty sure I was beyond saving.

He stood up. "I better let you get some rest, and I better get home. My wife is probably wondering what happened to me anyway—if she's not already asleep." He laughed and put his hand on my shoulder. For once, I didn't flinch at a touch.

I noticed the cut on his cheek. "You're bleeding." I pointed to the cut. "I'm so sorry, man, that I hurt you."

"It's nothing," he said as he wiped his cheek. He turned and walked to the door.

"Rev?" He stopped and turned toward me. "Thanks for everything."

"Anytime, my friend. Anytime."

After he left, the silence became deafening. The images from the dream, and even worse, from the real thing, crept back. I was restless, so I wandered the hallways. I found the sanctuary. It had been a long time since I stood at an altar. It was different than the Catholic church I'd grown up in—no Jesus on the crucifix or the Blessed Virgin staring at me. Yet I had the strange sensation that someone was watching. *Was it Robbie or the reverend or maybe God himself*, I wondered. I didn't know. But whoever it was, only one word echoed in my head.

Why.

I had no answer, and that emptiness had plagued me for years. Nothing had been able to keep the torment at bay except for the booze, and I knew then that I needed a drink. Bad. If I hadn't needed it so bad, I wouldn't have stopped at his office, and I wouldn't have scoured his desk for the money. With the handful of bills safely tucked in my pocket, I headed to the bar, desperate for a truce with the nightmares.

RICHARD

I USED TO GO to that church when I was a boy and I thought I might go back when that new preacher come to town. But as soon as I heard he was preaching all kinds of things that aren't in the Bible, I knew I'd never darken the door of that church again, at least as long as he was there.

TYLER

THE WORLD BEGAN TO change for me the day Mom and Dad brought Hannah home from the hospital. It was coincidence, I know now, that her arrival occurred just at the time I began to realize that I was different. For a while, even though it didn't make sense, I associated the feeling with Hannah's presence.

Of course it didn't have anything to do with her. I had just turned thirteen and it was a few more years before I understood that I'm gay. But back then I just knew what it felt like to be different than my friends at school and definitely from the boys at church. Anytime I had those thoughts—the thoughts that I knew I wasn't supposed to have—I pushed them down. They confused me because they felt so right, so genuine, but I couldn't imagine anyone, let alone my parents, understanding them.

There were times I thought about talking to Dad about it. I watched the way he was with people who were struggling to be good. Maybe he will understand, I told myself. But those were people who didn't go to church. They were people who could change once they were shown the right path. They weren't people who were supposed to already be on the path and they certainly weren't people who had to live up to the expectations of being the preacher's kid.

It didn't help that living in Mercy was like living in a glass bowl. Everyone knew everyone else's business, and of course they paid particular attention to ours. A couple of years after we moved there, kids at school started picking fights. Some would recount all of the people Dad had supposedly hurt and then tell me that we needed to go back where we came from. One girl told me that my dad was the devil and he was surely going to drag us to hell with him.

The first time it happened, when I was in the third grade, I came home crying. Mom sat me down and gently explained, as she always did, that just because someone says something doesn't make it so. That night, when Dad put me to bed, he said Mom had told him what happened.

"I wanted to punch Jimmy," I said. I was sure Dad would be pleased that I was ready to defend him.

"But you didn't, did you?"

"No." I hung my head, ashamed that I was a coward.

He lifted my chin with his finger and smiled at me.

"That's a good thing, Tyler," he said. "People are always going to say things and sometimes those things are going to be hurtful. Even Jesus had people saying bad things about him. Do you remember what he told us to do when people were like that?"

"Turn the other cheek?"

"That's right. It's okay to feel hurt if someone says those things, but instead of saying anything back—and especially instead of doing anything—just keep treating them nice." He gave me a hug. When he got to the door, he said "I love you" before turning off the light. At nine, I had no idea how I was supposed to do that, but I was determined not to disappoint him.

After Hannah was born, Dad was always busy at church. There were many times he wasn't there when I got home from school or when Mom put dinner on the table. She cried a lot back then, although she tried to hide it. I worried that Dad knew my secret, that maybe that was why he was staying away—because I had disappointed him. I hated the thought of it, but worse, I hated that I might be the reason Mom was crying.

Things got better for a while. One night, when Mom had taken Blake to soccer practice, Dad took me to get ice cream. For the first time in a long time, we laughed together, and I realized how much I had missed him, had missed being with him. I was content, at least until we got into the car to go home, when I was overcome with dread. I knew that if he ever knew my secret thoughts, it would never be this way again.

"Dad," I said, "would you still love me if I was a bad person?"

"What kind of question is that?" It wasn't just surprise in his voice, it was terror.

"I don't know. I guess I just need to hear your answer."

He put his hand on my shoulder and looked at me. I could have sworn I saw a tear at the corner of his eye. "I'll always love you no matter what."

I should have been comforted, but I wasn't.

REED

Grayson Armstrong was destroying the New Hope Baptist Church, and I was determined to preserve whatever little bit of it remained, maybe even restore it to what it used to be. I know a thing or two about restoration. I know what it means to recognize something special and to do everything in your power to bring it back to its former glory.

My dad's older brother, Billy, always had some restoration project going and, of course, I was usually right in the middle of it. If anyone was looking for us on a Saturday morning, they'd almost always find us in his basement trying to bring a broken radio back to life or refinish a beat-up, old table for Aunt Ruth.

My favorite project, though, was the 1940 LaSalle convertible. It was in horrible shape when Uncle Billy got it. The navy blue paint was not only faded but resembled the spots on a cow, and the front grill was bent from a collision with something much stouter. There was a big rip in the leather seat, and don't even get me started on the condition of the engine. Uncle Billy and I, and sometimes Dad, spent more than two years restoring that LaSalle. When it was finished, we drove that thing every time we got a chance.

On steamy summer days, we'd put the top down, waving to everyone as we cruised through Mercy. We were proud of that car, but more than that, we were gratified that car—one of the last of its kind—was being what it was meant to be.

Uncle Billy left that car to me when he passed. I treasure it because it reminds me so much of him. It takes me back to those summer days when we pulled into a slot at the Burger Shack and people would stare in envy of that beautiful shiny blue car, especially when Uncle Billy honked the horn to get Carl's attention. We didn't bother pushing the red button to place an order. Carl already knew it. It was always the same old thing—two double cheeseburgers, fries, and chocolate shakes. While we waited for the order, we turned up the radio and Uncle Billy would sing falsetto with the Four Seasons or a smooth, velvety baritone with Elvis until I was giggling like a little girl.

How I miss that man.

I'm glad he wasn't around, though. He would have hated to see what Grayson Armstrong was doing to the church he and Dad grew up in. If he was still here, though, he'd be the first to tell me that there was a restoration project with my name on it, particularly if he knew that Grayson let some vagrant spend the night in the church.

I guess Grayson thought he could get away with it. He might have, too, if Tom hadn't swung by the church on the way to work that morning. Tom told me that he wanted to grab some sheet music for a community choral concert. It had been a long time since the church had any need for the sheet music. I told Tom he ought to just take it all so that someone could get use out of it. He would never do it, though. I think he held out hope that one day Grayson would change his mind.

I'd been around long enough to know Grayson wasn't about to do that on anything.

When Tom got to the church, Grayson hadn't arrived yet and Effie had just gotten there. Tom said she looked flustered about him being there. He figured out why as soon as he saw the cot and the sweat pants in the choir room. Of course Effie didn't say anything. She and Fred were so blinded by Grayson's supposed charm that neither of them would have condemned him even if they found out he was Jack the Ripper. Tom should have come right out and asked her, but he's too timid to confront anyone.

Not me, though. As soon as Tom told me what he saw, I marched right down to the church to find out what was going on. Of course, Grayson tried to make excuses for turning the church into a homeless shelter. It was as infuriating as the conversation I'd had with him just a couple of days before, the day of that big storm.

That day I found him in the diner, as usual, working on his

sermon. I wondered why we even bothered providing him an office. I plopped down in the booth without even waiting for an invitation to join him.

"Reed. What a pleasant surprise." His tone told me that he felt otherwise.

"I won't take long. It looks like you're busy." I hoped my tone matched his. "Addie told me about the flag incident this summer. It's why they've stopped coming to church—if you even noticed they're not coming. You know you hurt the sweetest two people in the whole world."

"I have to do what I've been led to do," he said.

"And you're not even sorry, are you? You know it's not just your church." The prissy waitress came to the table, but I sent her away.

"I know it's not. It belongs to God."

He had a way of knowing exactly how to piss me off. "Don't give me that self-righteous crap. It might work on some people, but I see it for what it is. Sanctimonious bull crap." I pointed my finger in his face. "That church is full of people you've stepped all over. I'll be damned if I'll let you destroy it or them. If you try any more of this stuff, I'll get you before the deacons and we'll just see how long you'll be around."

"There's really no need for threats." The color drained from his face. I hoped this had finally caught his attention. Nothing else had. But that very night he turned the church into a homeless shelter. That convinced me that I was going to have to make good on the threat.

HANK

I PRAY FOR PEACE. In the name of the Father, the Son, and the Holy Ghost.

BLESSED ARE THE PEACEMAKERS

FRED

IT WAS NEARLY THREE weeks after Grayson let Hank stay at the church that Reed called a meeting of the deacons. I can't say that I was surprised. He had been strangely quiet since finding out about it, and I knew it could only mean one thing. He was gathering support for some dramatic move.

I tried to warn Grayson. A week before the meeting, I went to talk to him and Natalie. I arrived at his house a little before seven. Natalie had just put the baby down and was helping Blake with homework. Tyler was slouched in a chair playing a video game. Grayson was in his jeans and a superhero T-shirt, Captain America, I think. Even after six years, I was still somehow surprised by how young he really was.

"Thanks for letting me come over here." I sat on the sofa after moving a baby rattle out of the way.

"You said it was urgent."

"It is." I glanced at Tyler and Blake. Grayson understood my meaning, and sent the boys upstairs. When they were out of sight, Natalie came over and sat on the arm of the chair beside Grayson.

"It's about the deacons' meeting, I gather," he said.

"I'm afraid so." I had tried to come up with a delicate way of putting it, but instead I just blurted it out. "It seems that Reed's trying to get rid of you. I see that doesn't surprise you."

"He threatened as much a couple of weeks ago."

"A couple of weeks ago? Why didn't you say anything? We could have been talking to people, getting them on our side."

He shook his head. "I don't play those games. I just can't."

"I don't think you have a choice this time," I pleaded.

"You always have a choice, Fred." He set his jaw firm, and I knew that meant he was done on the subject. I looked at Natalie, hoping at least she would understand the seriousness of the situation, perhaps persuade him to do something. But she can be as hardheaded as he is sometimes and I could see it was useless to try to persuade either of them.

"I'll be all right," Grayson said when he walked me to the door.

"I hope so, Grayson. Just don't underestimate Reed."

"I never do." He flashed his usual pleasant smile.

Driving home, I thought about that smile. I suspect Jesus would have smiled like that. Not the Jesus of my youth or the one Brother Gillman was always preaching about—the one that rebuked people and turned over tables and chased money changers out of the temple with a whip. No, it would be the Jesus that Grayson made me see. The one who kept company with scoundrels and enjoyed himself so much that the religious folk accused him of gluttony. It was the one who spoke gently to women caught in adultery or drawing water from a well.

Of course even that Jesus was crucified by the religious leaders. Somehow I had to make sure that Grayson didn't suffer the same fate.

CHARLIE

In the week before the deacons' meeting, I got visits from Reed Hyden and Fred Taylor. They were both making their cases for getting rid of Grayson or keeping him. I can't say I was happy about being put in the middle of the tug-of-war. Fred's visit was unexpected, not because of the position he took—he was clearly a Grayson supporter—but because it wasn't like him to be that bold. But Reed's visit didn't surprise me at all. He'd been a vocal critic of Grayson for a long time. I have to admit that his arguments were pretty compelling.

Despite my dread of the meeting, I arrived early that night. My wife Maggie complains all the time for rushing her just so we can wait twenty minutes after we arrive at our destination, but I always say I'd rather be a little early than a little late. Since I had a few minutes to kill, I wandered into the sanctuary. From the time I was dedicated as a baby to the time I walked my daughter Elizabeth down the aisle, the familiarity of that space always took me back to pleasant remembrances.

I didn't bother turning on the lights because there was plenty coming through the windows to make me heartsick. The room was nearly unrecognizable from what it was six years before. The beautiful walnut pews, the ones where I sat as a boy counting letters in the bulletin to keep me from being bored, had been replaced by rows of black chairs, like they use in corporate conference rooms. The bulky wooden podium, the throne-like chairs, and the choir seats were no longer situated on the pulpit. Instead, a thin acrylic podium and a stool were perched on one side and a drum set, microphone stands, and amplifiers were on the other side.

The light from the street lamps illuminated the now white paneling and gave a glow to the painting of Jesus near the front of the church. There had always been a painting there—Jesus with a lamb cradled in his arm. The good shepherd. But that painting had been replaced with a modern one of Jesus's face. To tell the truth, I had never liked it—too modern for my taste. But that night, maybe because the way the light was hitting it, I was drawn to it. The wild mix of colors and shadows in the painting created the illusion of a face but the eyes were clear and penetrating. That night they were staring into my soul.

"I've always liked this painting," a voice came from the dark. It was Grayson. "He looks so weary."

"Weary?" I had never heard Jesus described that way.

"Yeah. So many paintings depict Jesus's divinity." I figured he was referring to the old painting and the halo of light surrounding Christ's head. "But I prefer the ones that show his humanity," Grayson continued. "When I see that weariness, I see the brokenness of the people around me. To tell you the truth, I see me."

"The least of these," I added, not really knowing where the thought came from.

"Exactly. I guess for me his divinity is understood. His humanity, though, is what connects him to us—and to each other." *Like a good shepherd*, I thought. We stood silently staring at the painting, and even when we left for the meeting, those eyes haunted me.

FRED

Reed thought he was being clever to hold the deacons' meeting in the choir room. I'm pretty sure he expected Grayson to wilt with shame sitting in the very room that he had supposedly desecrated. The tension in the room was palpable, but you'd never know it by Grayson. If everyone didn't know better, you would have thought it was just a regular meeting.

Reed had set up two folding conference tables end-to-end. He sat at one end and Grayson sat at the other. The rest of us lined the sides. In spite of the gravity of the meeting, I had to stifle an urge to laugh. With Reed and Grayson staring each other down at opposite ends of the table, it felt a little like a bad western, with us town folk nervously waiting for the first gun to be drawn. My amusement was short lived. Reed was the first to fire.

"Grayson Armstrong has been determined to make this church into some kind of progressive watered-down version of what it once was." Reed didn't take his eyes off of Grayson while he spoke. I didn't take my eyes of Reed. "I think it's time—long past time—to do something about it."

Samuel Griffin, who was sitting next to Reed, nodded in agreement. "We have lost many good members in the past six years."

"And gained many more," I added.

"At a huge cost," Reed glared at me. "You do realize how many people he's hurt, don't you?"

I looked at Grayson. His brow was furrowed but he didn't respond.

"A whole bunch," Roger Murphy said. The comment was directed at me. "My sister Agnes was one of them. She'd been teaching Sunday School for years and *he* drove her out of the church."

I was surprised that Roger would bring up Agnes. Maybe he didn't realize that I knew what really happened. That Agnes had been gossiping about Grayson—not just the "he's a bad pastor" kind of stuff but malicious insinuations about Grayson and other women. One day Effie overheard Agnes at the Food Fair and called her on it, which sent Agnes into a snit. She went right to the church and demanded that Grayson fire Effie. Agnes didn't bother to tell the whole story. Just as she was telling her version of what happened in the store—lies and all—Effie came in. Of course Grayson didn't know that he had also been slandered—and Effie wasn't about to tell him—but he did know that what Agnes was saying about Effie was a lie. He asked Agnes if she knew the Ten Commandments. She huffed out an indignant yes. "Perhaps, then, you might want to meditate on the ninth commandment." That's when she stormed out and never came back to the church again, though I'm sure her version of the story is very different.

I wondered if Grayson would correct Roger, but I could have guessed that he wouldn't. In fact, that whole night, he never responded to any of their accusations, even the one Reed had been saving until the right moment.

"I've tried to give him"—he wasn't even using his name by that time—"the benefit of the doubt, but you all know what he did a few weeks ago. Without even consulting with us, without getting approval from anyone, he turned this church into a homeless shelter. He let the town drunk stay unsupervised in this building—in this very room—apparently without a thought to what might happen."

"Nothing did happen," I said.

"This time," Reed snapped back.

"Besides, I was there and he *did* consult me," I added.

"And you think that makes it better?" Reed's face flushed. He stared at Grayson again."Well don't you have anything to say for yourself?"

Grayson paused for a long time and then finally said, "I believe my actions have spoken for me. You know that no words will matter here. So go ahead and do what you feel you must do."

That got Reed even more riled up. He turned to the other men. "Do you see how he is?" He glared at Grayson. "You're a pompous jerk and we can't let this go on any longer. We have the power to demand your resignation." Even though I knew this was probably coming, I lost my breath when the words made it a reality. Reed turned his attention to us. "To do that, I need a majority vote of this body. All those in favor…"

"Wait," Charlie Eversole said, barely above a whisper. He had been silent all night. He cleared his throat and then said the word again. Reed stopped and everyone looked at Charlie, who cleared his throat again before continuing. "I can't let you do this without saying my piece. Like many of you, I've struggled with the changes in this church. I'm not embarrassed to say that I've been to the point of tears at times because of it. But this is wrong. I might not have always agreed with Grayson, but he's a good man. And if he makes us a little uncomfortable sometimes so that we can open our eyes to 'the least of these,' well, I'm not so sure that's a bad thing." He looked at Grayson. "I'm sorry for my part in this. I hope you can forgive me."

"It's okay." Grayson whispered, not taking his eyes off Charlie.

A silence fell over the room and I thought maybe that it was over. But it wasn't. Not by a long shot.

NATALIE

When he got home, Grayson sank onto the old recliner with a loud sigh. He let his head fall back, casting his eyes upward, as if he was praying. Perhaps he was. I certainly had been while he was at the meeting. My Catholic friends pray the rosary at such times, but I knit. The repetition of stitches and rows are my meditation. I had quite a lengthy meditation that night, as the knitted rows spilled over my lap and over the seat cushion.

I laid my knitting beside me on the couch and studied Grayson's face—its long, oval shape, its straight and slender nose, its thin, pale lips. The hair that framed it was as black as the day we met with only a hint of gray at his temples to remind me that he was almost forty and that we had been together nearly half our lives.

We met in college when I was a part-time receptionist at a women's clinic that offered abortion services on Tuesdays. On those days, protesters gathered on the sidewalk in front of the clinic. Most of them quietly held their signs or offered to pray with women who were walking into the clinic. But a few shouted at them and some even tried to block their path to the clinic doors. The women who made it in, who didn't turn back in panic, were shaken. "They don't know. They don't understand," the women often said, with tears running down their cheeks.

One day three young men, Grayson included, showed up to escort women into the clinic. The clinic director agreed to it, but warned them that he didn't want any confrontations with the protestors. The guys agreed, and I watched all afternoon as they took turns walking past the protesters to the parking lot and placing themselves between the protesters and the woman on the return trip. Even when a protester yelled at them or called them names, the guys continued undaunted, sometimes even throwing a smile in the direction of the protester.

I was captivated by Grayson almost from the start. I watched him intently, though I was quick to turn away if he caught me looking. But even then, I'd see him smile at me, and maybe I glimpsed a hint of a blush in his cheeks. If it had just been his good looks, I probably would have tired of him quickly. But I was drawn to the easy-going, gentle way he had with people, especially with the frightened women. I would overhear him reassure each of the women as she made it inside the door. "You're safe now," he'd say. She would look up at him and ask, "Weren't you scared?" He'd smiled at her. "A little, but I try not to let fear control me." Most of the time she'd nod and smile back with gratitude. "Take care of yourself," he'd say as he left her at the reception desk, knowing that her biggest anguish was probably not the protesters but her own self-doubt.

It took a few months before Grayson finally asked me out. At dinner, he was more fidgety than I expected given the confident charm I had observed for weeks. He told me later that he knew he wanted to marry me soon after we met, so he was terrified of bungling that first date. He shouldn't have been. I was already spellbound. Yet I was still intrigued about one thing. I had chosen to work at the clinic in spite of—or maybe because of—my beliefs. But I wondered why he was involved.

"So I'm curious," I said. "What made you start coming to the clinic?"

"My buddies and I saw on the news what was happening at the clinic. We knew it wasn't right, so we decided to do something about it."

"So do you believe abortion is okay?" I worried that the question was too blunt.

"It's not a matter of what I believe about abortion. It's a matter of what I believe about God." He leaned forward. "But my faith isn't about believing, it's about doing. God says to learn to do right and to seek justice and defend the oppressed."

I looked down at the table and fumbled with my napkin.

"You seem surprised."

"I guess I just assumed you weren't a believer." In my shame, I couldn't look at him.

"Actually, there was a time a couple of years ago when I didn't believe in God."

"You were an atheist?" I had never met one before.

"I didn't really identify myself like that, but yeah I guess I was."

"So what changed?"

"I finally realized that my beef wasn't with God but with some people who claimed to speak in his name. That helped me come to peace with God." He paused and then grinned. "I'm still working on coming to peace with some of those people who claim to speak in his name."

The memory of those words echoed as I stared at Grayson. He was weary from the years of struggle. I could read it on his face.

"I take it the meeting didn't go well," I finally said.

"Actually, it went better than I expected. Charlie Eversole really surprised me tonight. Made me feel hopeful for the church for the first time in a long time. Reed tried to get the vote anyway, but it was seven to five against him."

"Wow. That's a bit unexpected." I was surprisingly relieved. "So we're staying?"

"For now." He looked at me. "Is that okay?" He knew that it had been harder for me to settle into the small town.

"Yeah." I walked to the recliner and snuggled in beside him. "I'll always be right here beside you—no matter what."

"That means a lot." He reached his arm around me and pulled me closer. "Because I don't think Reed's done yet. I suspect the worst is yet to come."

"Aren't you afraid of what'll he'll do?"

"I'm more worried about you and the kids." He looked at me. "But I can't be afraid. Not when I know there's still so much more to do. I just have to keep pushing it away."

I laid my hand on his chest. As the dread and doubt escaped from his body, they found a home in mine and settled in.

ADDIE

He never did come visit. Not once. After Ollie and I left the church, Brother Armstrong never came to check on us. Oh, I ran into him a few times around town when we were shopping or at the park. He was friendly enough, but he never once asked why we left or offered a way for us to come back. He never even came to the funeral when Ollie passed—not even the visitation. When we saw each other at the grocery store a few weeks after, he asked how I was doing and told me how sorry to hear that Ollie had passed away, but by then it was too late to show sympathy as far as I was concerned. It was all I needed to know to see what kind of man he was. There were some people that thought he hung the moon, but he was never half the man my Ollie was.

I try to never speak ill of anyone, so I'll just leave it at that.

HANK

I'm not one to get into bar room brawls, but I sure as hell got into one that night after mouthing off to some jackass. I don't even remember what it was about, but it was probably some pointless trash talk—something I'm prone to do after a few drinks. Most of the time I can hold my own when it comes to a fight, but three of them ganged up on me and I got my ass kicked. Might have met my maker if the bartender didn't yank those guys off of me. The cold tile floor felt good for a while, so I just lay there to catch my breath. Anyway, no one bothered to check on me. I'm sure I deserved that. I was finally picking myself up off the floor when a hand reached down to help me. I looked up to see the Reverend's face.

It had been several months since I'd seen him. To tell the truth, I had been avoiding him. Never in my life had I taken anything that wasn't mine. My mother taught me better than that. I may have bummed a dollar or two from someone or maybe even charmed my way to getting a bottle off of someone. But I never stole—until I did from him. So he was the last person I wanted to see.

"Looks like you could use a friend," he said as he helped me to my feet.

I didn't tell him that I had no interest in being friends. Lost too many of them through the years to care about making new ones. But the pain in my jaw and my left side was beginning to force its way past the liquor so I at least took his help. He led me to a table in the back of the room and I eased onto a chair.

"I think you lost your way, Reverend. Won't hanging out in bars get you kicked out of your church?"

He laughed. "Maybe. But where else would a surgeon be but in the operating room? Besides, I haven't seen you in a while. The guys said you've not been around the old factory much."

"Yeah, I just needed some time alone." The truth was, I had

been piss-ass drunk for most of the time. Better to numb the mind than to continue to conjure the past—a past that never ends well. I wondered if the reverend could ever understand the beast in my mind, but I was pretty sure no preacher could, not even this one. Hell, even I couldn't.

We were quiet for a bit. It was hard anyway to talk over the guys gathered around the bar television, cheering every big play. I had been watching the game before the fight, so I leaned back to see the score but jerked forward just about as quick when a sharp pain ran down my side.

"You're in pain," the reverend said. I almost blurted out "No shit" but I caught myself. Instead I just nodded.

"Maybe I should take you to the ER."

"No thanks. I don't like hospitals or doctors. Maybe another drink would help. It's the best medicine."

"I think you've had enough for tonight," he said. He was probably right, but I didn't need or want a babysitter either. "Let me take you to get something to eat instead."

"I'm in no condition to get out anywhere." I really didn't feel like moving.

"We don't have to get out. We can go to the drive-in and get a burger."

I hadn't eaten much for a couple of days, certainly no meat, so I had to admit that a burger sounded good.

At the Burger Shack, I scarfed down the double cheeseburger in just a few minutes. It wasn't until I popped in the last bite that I was aware again of the pain in my jaw. It was a reminder that I had acted stupidly in the bar—but then again that was nothing new for me.

"Why are you so interested in a worthless piece of shit like me?" I asked the reverend, who was sipping on a shake. I was dead serious, but he laughed.

"Sorry, Hank, but I've never heard anyone describe himself that way." And then he looked at me, more thoughtful. "In all seriousness, I don't think you and I are all that different."

"Come on, Rev. We're nothing alike."

"No, really. We're both running from our past—trying to hide from it, or more to the point, from our feelings about it."

"What the hell could you be running from? A badly overdue library book?" I laughed and expected him to as well. He didn't, though he did smile.

"Oh, I have a few thousand of those kinds of stories for sure." He looked in my direction but stared past me, awakening, I imagine, some distant memory. "But there are some things far worse back there. I speak from experience that the guilt can eat you up." He lingered with the memory for a few seconds before turning his attention back to me. "I can't pretend to understand what your demons are—the things that keep you running—but I do understand the effects of shame and regret. I also know what it's like to feel like a fraud."

I had the strange sensation of being on the wrong side of a confessional. If he was looking for absolution, he had gone to the wrong person. I certainly was in no position to offer it.

We sat in awkward silence while I finished my fries. I knew I should say something, that he was probably expecting me to say something. What could I say, though? I had never heard a preacher say such things. Grayson Armstrong had always struck me as different—more real—than any religious person I'd ever known. But maybe this was too real. Finally, I just cleared my throat and murmured a quick "I'm sorry, man." He acknowledged with a whispered "thanks" but he was probably disappointed that I didn't say more.

When I finished eating, he offered to drop me anywhere I wanted to go. I suppose I should have gone back to the factory because I hadn't seen the guys in a while. But I'd had a strong urge to be alone for quite a while. I had been staying quite a bit at a pavilion in the park, when I didn't get chased off by the cops, so I told him to drop me there.

When we stopped at the pavilion, I looked at him, trying to figure him out. It had been a strange night. "Thanks for helping me at the bar tonight and for the meal," I said.

"I hate leaving you here," he said.

“I’ll be okay,” I replied as I got out of the car. “And so will you,” I added. But watching his car drive away, I wasn’t at all sure either of us would be.

TOM

To say that Grayson Armstrong destroyed my faith gives him too much credit. That's not to say, though, that he didn't shake it to its very foundations. Unlike Reed, who seemed to see the chinks in the armor within a couple of months, I didn't see Grayson for what he was until it was too late.

He'd been at the church a little more than two years when the trouble really started brewing. There had been lots of changes, slow at first and then coming with greater frequency. Of course, that was difficult for some people. Each time complaints bubbled to the surface, I defended Grayson. I didn't see how people could argue with the results. After all, we had been a church on the verge of dying, but we'd seen significant growth in the two years since Grayson came, despite losing some families who couldn't handle the change. But that didn't stop people from picking nits, and I grew tired of the constant complaints. They were just being childish as far as I was concerned, and I told Reed as much. He laughed.

"You'll eat your words, Tom, and I sure hope I'm around to see it when you do."

He was—but he had to wait another two years to get that satisfaction.

That night is etched in my memory, a terrible scene on a perpetual loop. Over and over, I see the conference room just on the other side of Grayson's office. I see the two six-foot folding tables pushed together to accommodate everyone for the weekly staff meeting. I see the startled faces of everyone after I burst into the room twenty minutes late. I feel the heaviness of the room, like every bit of the air has been sucked out when I open the door. I catch Reed staring at me and he smiles—smirks, really. There is an "I told you so" in his eyes, though it doesn't register at the time.

"Sorry I'm late," I say as I plop onto an empty chair. "I got caught at work."

"No problem," Grayson says, his voice missing its usual warmth. "We were just talking about a change—" He pauses and clears his throat. "—a change that will affect you."

"Oh...okay." I hope no one can hear the tremor in my voice, especially Reed.

Grayson stares at the paper in front of him for a few seconds and then looks back at me.

"We really appreciate all you've done to lead the music and the choir...for how long now?"

"Twenty years."

"Yes, twenty years. That's a long time." He pauses again, more hesitant than I'd ever seen him. I just want him to say whatever he's going to say. "As you know," he finally starts again, "the church is growing and the demographics have really changed." I nod. "So we've decided to go in a different direction with the worship service."

"Different direction?" I'm still confused. It hasn't occurred to me yet what he's really saying. Even when he tells me that they want to use a praise band all the time, even when he tells me that the church has grown big enough for a full-time worship minister, even when he explains that he has offered Kendall Murphy the position, I still struggle to process everything. I don't hear anything else at the staff meeting, and I definitely don't look at Reed. I'm sure he is trying to catch my eye again, to gloat over everything he'd been trying to tell me—everything that I had dismissed as pettiness.

As soon as the staff meeting is over, I want to get out of there as quick as I can. Before I can get to the door, Grayson stops me.

"Tom, I'm sorry you found out this way. I'd planned to speak to you before the meeting."

I don't want to talk to him. I don't know what to say to him—or what he expects me to say to him. So I just say, "It's okay. I'm okay."

"I hope so." He puts his hand on my shoulder and I resist the urge to jerk away from his touch. Instinctively, he lowers his hand and takes a step back. "Anyway, I'm here if you want to talk about it."

I nod and we shake hands, and then I'm out the door. I see Reed standing with someone in the parking lot, but I walk by without acknowledging them.

On the drive home, I'm still trying to process the evening. As I replay every word, my mind drifts back to a Saturday night a few months ago, to a very different conversation with Grayson.

As usual, I found myself alone at the church to prepare for Sunday services. I liked to take advantage of the quiet by praying and meditating on the songs I'd selected for the next day. Sometimes I would slip into the dark sanctuary, turn on the piano lamp, and play some old hymns, letting the music fill the empty space—the way it always did inside of me.

That night, after playing two or three hymns, my fingers fell into the familiar, comfortable rhythms of "It Is Well with My Soul." I can't play that song, I can't sing those words without thinking of the story behind the song's creation, without thinking about the hope that pushed past the sorrow. I can't sing it without feeling every word. So when Grayson appeared unexpectedly, catching me in full vibrato midway through the final verse, I was both startled and embarrassed.

"Don't stop on my account," he said from the dark. "That was beautiful."

"Thanks. I get carried away with that song sometimes."

"Nonsense. I think that's what I enjoy most about your singing." He stepped into the small circle of light surrounding the piano. "You love to sing, don't you?"

It seemed like a strange question, but it was easy to answer. "Oh my, yes. Ever since I can remember. My mother said that I came out of the womb singing." We laughed. "She told me my voice was a gift from God and whatever else I did, if I wasn't praising God with it, then it showed a lack of gratitude."

"Well, you were certainly praising him tonight. That's one of my favorite hymns."

"Then sing it with me."

"Oh no. I'm not a musician like you."

"Music is not just in your mouth. It's in your heart. You have a heart, don't you?" I smiled at him.

"I hope so," he said softly.

As we sang, leaving every inhibition on the floor and just feeling the music, I also felt the kinship music can bring.

And now, as I drive home, I wonder how I could have misunderstood that kinship. How could I have been so wrong about Grayson? With no answer coming to mind, I am empty—and for the first time in my life, there is no music to fill the emptiness.

RAMIE

I STOOD STARING AT the door to the church for several minutes, trying to decide if I would go in. I had promised myself that I would never set foot in a church again, not after what Mommy did to me and Daddy. Not after she tried to beat the devil out of me and then turned around and run off with the preacher. Daddy was mad as hell at the preacher, but as much as he had threatened to leave, Daddy was brokenhearted when she was the one that took off.

I had never told the whole story to anyone, and certainly not a preacher. So when Grayson offered to talk with me, to hear my story, I was skeptical. I couldn't help but wonder what he expected out of it. Yet there I was, standing at the church door.

"It was hard for you to come here today, wasn't it?" he said after I was seated in his office. I guess he understood the surprise on my face because he continued. "It's been months since I extended the invitation."

My face flushed and I looked away. "I thought about coming hundreds of times, but I was…too nervous. That's silly, isn't it?"

"Not really. Sometimes talking about ourselves is the scariest thing to do. But let me assure you, we'll only talk about what you want to talk about—and whenever you're done, we're done."

He leaned forward, his warm eyes reminding me again of my daddy. "It's okay," I could hear Daddy whisper through those eyes. So I took a deep breath, sunk back into the chair, and let the story start spilling out—a story that always seemed to start and stop with my mother.

Mommy was different before she got religion. The day I turned seven was one of the best days of my life. She was waiting for me when I got off the school bus, which she didn't do too often. I was so excited that I ran to her. She threw open her arms and when I reached her, she scooped me up and twirled around. I squealed with delight as I watched the houses and trees swirl around me. When she finally stopped, she hugged me tight. I snuggled against her neck, letting her perfume survive in my memory. "Happy birthday, baby girl," she whispered in my ear.

That night we had a party—just her and Daddy and me. When Mommy lit the candles on my cake, I stopped for a second to memorize her face, softened by the candle light, as if somehow I could sense change coming. I didn't understand it then, but I became convinced that it was a premonition. I've had a few since then. But that night, I just cherished the moment not really understanding why.

I didn't get any presents—Mommy and Daddy couldn't afford any—but it didn't matter to me. The only present I ever really wanted was for Daddy to play his guitar, so I begged him to play that night. He pretended he was too tired, but then he laughed and snatched his guitar from behind the couch. Mommy and I clapped along as he played a couple of old rock and roll songs. Daddy always said the old songs were the best. I liked them too, which is why he knew what I was waiting to hear. Daddy did the best Johnny Cash imitation. So when he began "Ring of Fire," I squealed and twirled around. He winked at Mommy when he sang "bound by wild desire." She blushed, the way she sometimes did when he looked at her like that, but I knew she was under his spell. We both were. If I had known what was coming, I would have wished that we were frozen in that moment forever.

But, of course, we weren't.

It wasn't long after that she found religion—or maybe it was that she rediscovered it. She told me once that she had grown up in the church but that she rebelled as a teenager. And then she met Daddy, who was never what you'd call a believer, and she thought she had left religion for good. Until a pale, red-headed preacher came to the house to invite the family to the revival meeting at the church down the road. Daddy laughed at the invitation after the preacher left, but Mommy looked strange, and without telling anyone, she went to the first night of the revival. She went again the next night, this time telling Daddy where she was going. He didn't try to stop her, but he did tease her about it. She gave him a disapproving look as she picked up her purse. "Don't, John, please," she whispered as she dabbed away a tear and walked out the door. Daddy was frozen for a moment. Even then, I think we both knew it was over.

By the fourth night of the revival, Mommy dragged me to church with her. It was a strange place, at least to a seven-year-old, but the people were friendly. Brother Reynolds, the preacher, tweaked my cheek and told me he was glad to see me. And then he looked up at Mommy and smiled in a way that made me uncomfortable. But she smiled back.

Before the service began, Mommy walked us down toward the front and we sat on the hard pews. A few people close by looked at us and smiled, but I didn't really like the attention and just clung tighter to her. As the service started, a couple of men got up to speak, including Brother Reynolds. His words echoed against the bare walls and bounced off the wooden floor so that I was forced to cover my ears—before Mommy pulled my hands down and gave me a stern look. I bowed my head and tried not to think about the words bouncing around the room but concentrated instead on the worn patent leather shoes, which were just a little too big for me, that Mommy had gotten from the clothes closet at the church.

When the singing started, I felt my body relax. The rhythms and the harmonies were comforting—not quite the same way that Daddy's signing was, but I began to think that maybe church wasn't going to be so bad. I could hear Mommy singing, her voice joining the others, soft yet confident. She had always been self-conscious about her signing. But I loved her voice, especially when she and Daddy sang together.

I looked up at her, searching for the soft lines in her face, the ones I had seen the night of my birthday. She looked down and I caught a glimpse of them before she focused again on the man waving his arms at the front of the church. It was one of the last times I saw them. Even when she was baptized two nights later, when she rose from the water, her long brown hair dripping down the white robe, her face bore the full weight of the depravity she was now obligated to oppose.

Daddy and I were stark reminders of that depravity. He, of course, because he was an unbeliever, though she couldn't really do anything about that. Daddy was a stubborn man. But she could do something about me. The first time I remember Mommy taking the belt to me was when I slipped out of church and walked home by myself. Every time she hit me with the belt, I could feel the frantic rage—I could hear the tears of relief become cries of wrath and shame. The beatings were always worse after a protracted meeting, when she was fired up for God.

I was ten when Mommy left. She wasn't there when I came home from school. Daddy searched for her, called everyone he knew to call—even the police. And then we began hearing the rumors, that she and Brother Reynolds had left town together. I thought Daddy would be happy, but he was inconsolable. I knew then that I had to make it right for him—and I did eventually. I was his rock and he was mine until he died when I was sixteen. Even though he was very sick before he died, I'll always believe it was from a broken heart.

Standing over his grave, I thought back to my seventh birthday and him singing those old songs. But as I stared at his name etched into that stone, it was my mother's voice I heard. After I had gone to bed that night, she and Daddy kept singing and as I drifted off to sleep, I could hear her melancholy voice.

I'm just a poor wayfaring stranger.
While journeying through this world of woe;
Yet there's no sickness, toil, or danger
In that bright land to which I go.
I know dark clouds will gather round me,
I know my way is hard and steep;
Yet brighter fields lie just before me,
Where God's redeemed their vigils keep.

The memory was deep and painful and I couldn't—wouldn't—take it further. I was done. When my eyes met Grayson's, I was surprised that he was crying. "I'm so very sorry, Ramie," he said. I tried to respond, but I guess I had used up all of my words. "After everything you've been through, I don't mean this to sound like I don't understand your pain, but I think the healing you're looking for can only be found in God."

That made my defenses build back. "I told you before. I have no interest in church," I said as nicely as I could.

"I'm not talking about church, Ramie," he said. "In fact, I don't want you to go to church." I was confused, but I waited for him to continue. "I'm talking about discovering the Father—apart from the church, apart from religion. It won't happen in a day, or perhaps even a year. It's a journey. One that I'm still on myself."

He reached into his desk and brought out a worn Bible. And then he walked around and sat down beside me. "I want you to have this." I shook my head. "Please," he said as he placed it into my hands. "Whenever you're ready, start with the bookmarked page." He smiled and I reluctantly accepted it.

I hadn't planned on opening it, so when I got home I just threw it down onto the table beside the couch. I fixed a cup of tea and sat down to watch some TV. But something in Grayson's look always took me back to my daddy and a longing for one of Daddy's comforting hugs. I stared at the book for a minute and after chasing away the ghost of my mother, I picked up the book. I fumbled to the bookmarked page and found a highlighted passage. *He heals the brokenhearted and binds up their wounds. He determines the number of the stars and calls them each by name. Great is our Lord and mighty in power; his understanding has no limit.*

I closed the book and cradled it to my chest. As I looked into the night sky, I thought I heard someone whisper my name.

JILL

Grayson was disappointed when we left Ignite. I could see it in his eyes. But I told him when he came to visit us that it had nothing to do with him. I wished like anything we could have stayed, but Brad and I were tired of the church politics. When our youngest daughter wanted to start going to the Methodist church where her best friend went, it made the decision easier.

I know that some people in town have given him a hard time, like he's the devil himself. But I've always believed that change is good—and necessary most of the time. I told Grayson that. I told him that I wished we could have stayed and helped him. He needed counterbalance to all the negativity, and I sure hated to cause him more hurt. He was such a good man. Such a man of God.

TYLER

My DAD SAW GOD in the small, everyday acts of ordinary people. God was real and tangible to him. For me, God—if he exists—is in the vastness of the ocean or the stars in the night sky. He is detached and distant. The smallness of our lives are inconsequential, so how can he care about what happens to each of us? I'm convinced our happiness means nothing to him, least of all my happiness. Dad tried to assure me that God does care, but the truth of the matter was, I wasn't convinced Dad cared either. I certainly hadn't made it easy for him to care.

My teenage years were a challenge for us both. He was an unyielding rocky coastline and I was the relentless waves that pounded against it. We were forces of nature locked in an age-old battle of wills. "I hate being your son," I said to him once. "You have no idea how hard it is." I could see the hurt in his eyes and, for a minute, I was actually glad. It wasn't really fair, but I was just so angry with him for being who he was—for being a pastor, especially one that stirred the pot, even if it was for the right reasons. Everything he did, everything he said became a millstone for me, weighing down until I could barely breathe. The only way I knew to resist was to shove against it as hard as I could. It wasn't until I met Kevin during my freshman year of high school that I learned how hard I was willing to shove.

Kevin was in my English and PE classes. He was older than the rest of us because he'd been held back a year. That made him dangerous, at least most everybody thought so. Maybe that was because he already had his driver's license or because he used words that would make a sailor blush. Or maybe it was just because he always looked like he was about to punch someone.

"I hear he spent some time in juvie. He's bad news," Rachel told me. She'd been my best friend since fourth grade, and I usually listened to her. But something in Kevin's dark, brooding nature was familiar. It was like looking at one of those fun-house mirrors, seeing a distorted image but knowing it was you in there somewhere. I had to get to know Kevin if I wanted to know myself.

It wasn't easy to get Kevin's attention. I figured it was because he knew I was a PK, so he must have thought I was going to judge him or, worse yet, try to save him. He didn't need to worry. I was in no position to judge anyone, and even though I'd been saved myself—baptized when I was ten—I hadn't felt close to God in a while. Kevin, on the other hand, awakened feelings I didn't even know I had. They were frightening but at the same time they were powerful.

The first few times I attempted to make friends with him he treated me like I was his annoying kid brother who was trying to tag along. But toward the end of the school year he surprised me by inviting me to a party at his cousin's house. I was so excited that I didn't bother asking any questions or waiting to get permission from my parents. My quick—and perhaps too enthusiastic "yes"—made Kevin laugh. I probably blushed, but I tried to cover up my embarrassment by laughing as well.

I lied to Mom and Dad about the party. It wasn't the first lie I'd ever told them but it certainly was the biggest. They would have never let me go if they had known that Kevin's cousin was twenty-five or that the party was in a run-down part of town—not the worst part of town, but certainly not where my parents would have wanted me if they had known. Not that I was that keen on it either, but I was pretty sure that it would be my only opportunity to develop a friendship with Kevin, so I convinced myself it was worth the risk.

On the night of the party, I had my dad drop me off at the movies. I told him that Rachel wanted to see the new superhero movie and even though I'd already seen it I agreed to go with her—which wasn't a total lie. I told him we'd probably hang out for a while after the movie. Once Dad was out of sight, I walked the half mile or so to the address Kevin had given me.

The neighborhood had probably been charming when these bungalow houses were built in the 1920s. It was hard to imagine what it must have been like back then when they were new and neighbors gathered on each other's front porches swapping stories and waving to the young families as they strolled by with baby carriages. But the houses that were once vibrant had been neglected for years. I stood in front of number 337. Even in the twilight, I could see that the paint on the graying siding and decorative trim was peeling or gone altogether. A number of slats from the porch railing had disappeared and chunks of concrete were missing from the edges of the front steps. *Maybe this was a mistake*, I thought. *Maybe I should just turn around and go watch a movie*. But the thought of Kevin being inside that house made me forget about any common sense I might have possessed.

When I got to the front door, which was open, I could hear music and voices toward the back of the house. With no visible doorbell, I gave a gentle knock on the screen door. No one seemed to notice, so I knocked again louder and then again when no one still came to the door.

"Quit your damn knocking and come the fuck in," someone finally called out.

I stepped inside and let my eyes adjust to the dim light. The house smelled musty, a bit like my grandma's house, except for the faint odor of alcohol, cigarettes, and what I assumed was pot coming from the back deck. Only the thought of Kevin propelled me forward. I passed through the living room and kitchen to the deck and was surprised to find only a couple of guys there.

"Hi," I mumbled. "I'm Tyler, a classmate of Kevin's." The guy holding a beer gave me a blank look. "He said I could come," I added.

"Oh, yeah. I remember him saying something about that. I'm Steve and this is Craig." Craig took a long draw on a cigarette while giving a quick nod in my direction. "Kevin's not here yet. Grab a beer and make yourself at home."

I felt more like an outsider than I usually did, but there was no turning back at that point. I picked up a beer. Trying desperately to fit in, I opened it and took a sip, beating down the urge to gag, and ducked into the corner of the deck near the house. Steve and Craig went back to talking like I wasn't there. I took a few more sips of the beer and tried to numb the fear that Kevin had set me up. Thankfully, it wasn't long before Kevin arrived with some other guys.

"Hey, Tyler," he called to me. "I see you're already one up on us. I guess I need to catch up." He laughed and raised a bottle, like a toast, to me. Whether it was the beer or Kevin's presence, I couldn't say, but I began to relax. When Kevin asked, I didn't hesitate to participate in the beer pong they'd set up. By the end of the game, with a few more drinks in me, I was whooping and calling out obscenities like I'd been doing it all my life. But I was also starting to feel dizzy and a little disoriented, so I excused myself from the next game and walked out into the yard. It was dark by this time, particularly away from the porch lights. The air was chilly, which helped shake loose the disorientation. I was staring up at the moon when I felt an arm around my shoulder.

"Are you all right, Tyler?" It was Kevin. I felt his breath near my face and my body responded. "I've been looking for you," he whispered in my ear.

I turned to him. "I'm right here," I said. He leaned toward me. I smelled the alcohol mixed with cigarette smoke as his mouth moved closer to mine. I was overcome by a bewildering but somehow comfortable desire, and I knew I *wanted* him to kiss me. Just as our lips were about to touch, he leaned back and laughed.

"I knew it! I just knew it! You're a faggot." I stared at him, fighting back the tears that were rushing to the surface. "Hey guys," he called toward the porch, "we've got ourselves a faggot here." My embarrassment melted quickly into panic as I realized that I didn't really know these guys, didn't know what they were capable of. I ran toward the porch and shoved my way past them. As I ran through the house and out the front door, I could hear their laughter, and above it all, I could hear Kevin calling, "Where are you going, fag boy? Come back and let me fuck you."

I ran down the dark street until I couldn't breathe. My stomach was churning and I felt chilled. The darkness bore down on me as my terror rose. I huddled near a parked car and did the only thing I knew to do—get out my cell phone and call my dad.

"You're where?" Dad said.

"Over on Green Street. Can you come get me?"

"What are you doing there? Where's Rachel?"

"Please, Dad. Just come get me."

"I'll be right there. Stay on the phone with me until I get there."

We talked, though neither of us were really saying anything—just words—as we were each trying to keep ourselves calm. When I saw the headlights, I stood up, hoping it was really him.

"Are you okay?" he asked when I got into the car.

"Yeah."

"What happened to you?"

"I don't want to talk about it," I said as we drove past Steve's house. So we were quiet. In the dark, as houses and streetlights slid past, the anger and embarrassment mixed with relief and tried to bubble its way to the surface through tears. I refused to let it.

When we got home, Mom was waiting at the door. She tried to hug me, and I felt her heart beating fast. I pulled away. As much as I wanted to feel safe in her arms, I couldn't face her—face them—at that moment.

"I'm going to bed," I said.

"Wait—" Dad called to me, but I was already up the stairs.

When I came down around eleven the next morning to eat and to take something for my head, I was hoping everyone would be gone, but Dad was in the kitchen. Just as I started to go back upstairs, he called to me.

"You were drunk when I picked you up last night," he said. He laid his book down and took off his reading glasses.

"So?" I said, looking him straight in the face. My head was pounding, but I was not about to let him know it.

"So? Is that all you have to say?" His voice was hard. The panic from the night before was gone.

"It wouldn't make a difference to you anyway." I really didn't want to talk about it, especially not with him.

"I'm so tired of that attitude of yours. Sometimes it makes me just want to slap you."

"Then go ahead. What's stopping you?" I shouted.

He didn't. I knew he wouldn't. Instead he just stared at me with his jaw set and his eyes glaring. After he sent me to my room—with me stomping my way there and slamming the door—I sank onto my bed. The tears that I had fought all night were not going to be stopped this time. I wasn't sure how I was ever going to face anyone again—not Kevin or the other kids at school, who I'm sure were going to find out what happened, or even Rachel. Somehow I was going to have to find a way, even if it meant burying my feelings so deep that even I couldn't find them. I knew the first thing I had to do was dry up my tears. *Boys don't cry*, I told myself.

As I wiped my eyes, I thought about how Dad had glared at me. His eyes reflected what I had just learned, that anger and fear are so closely related that we often mistake one for the other. He was afraid, and for the first time, I recognized myself in him.

EFFIE

"Is Grayson here?" A tentative voice said from the doorway. I looked up to see a woman in a simple white T-shirt and ripped jeans, a fashion trend I've never been able to understand. I seriously doubted it really was a fashion choice in her case, though. Her flip flops, which barely showed beneath the jeans that were too long, exposed dusty feet that were too small for those shoes. Her hair was in a ponytail and she stared at me with hollow brown eyes. As she cleared her throat, she looked embarrassed. "I mean Rev. Armstrong. Is the reverend here?"

"It's just Grayson around here, honey," I smiled at her. "He stepped out for a few minutes. He shouldn't be too much longer. You're welcome to wait if you like."

She just kept standing in the doorway like a statue—afraid to come in and afraid to go out.

She was a rather homely young woman and I didn't recognize her until she plopped onto the chair next to the door and let out an exasperated puff of air. She was the girl that worked in the diner across the street from the church. I'd been over there a few times, mainly just to track down Grayson, who seemed to live over there. To tell the truth, I dreaded going over there because of her. Her face always carried a moody expression, like she had sucked on a pile of lemons, like she was ready to spit in the food before serving it. I said that to Grayson once, but he just shook his head.

"She's not that bad," he said.

"Still, I make it a point to avoid people like that."

But there she sat in my office.

Her arms and legs were crossed so tight that I wondered if they might suddenly spring loose like a jack-in-the box. At some point, she did let one of the legs free to bounce in an uneasy staccato rhythm. Made me jumpy just watching her. A couple of times I saw her eye the clock and then the door, like she was calculating an escape plan. I kept wishing she would. We were both relieved when we heard the chime on the outside door. As soon as Grayson came into the office, her eyes lit up, bringing her whole face to life. As her smile spread, I could see a beauty there I hadn't seen before.

"Ramie, this is an unexpected pleasure," Grayson said. He didn't just shake her hand but grasped it with both of his and held onto it. "What brings you here?"

She glanced at me and her smile faded. She looked down at the floor before muttering "I don't know."

"It's okay," Grayson said, still holding onto her hand.

She looked back at him and again I saw her body relax. "I guess I just need to talk to someone, that's all."

"Then let's talk." He gave her hand a squeeze before dropping it to lead her into his office.

They were in there for nearly two hours—not that I was surprised. Grayson never seemed to rush anyone out of his office, even when I knew he was supposed to be somewhere else. When they did come out, her eyes and nose were red—even *his* eyes were red. She had a tissue in one hand and a worn Bible in the other. In spite of that, she gave Grayson a quick hug.

"Thank you," Ramie whispered, but I was close enough to hear. "Have a good day," she said to me as she walked out the door with a smile on that red, puffy face.

"I'm just amazed at the change in her since she came in," I said to Grayson after she left. "You have such an instinct in dealing with people."

He chuckled.

"No, it's not instinct at all. I'm just like everyone else—my natural tendency is to be quick to judge and quick to anger. It's just that I learned a long time ago that it's a spiritual discipline to look past the protective layer people put on—the layer that can be so infuriating to deal with—to see who they really are underneath. To begin to understand the pain that builds that protective layer one experience at a time takes patience." He looked at me and grinned. "Of course sometimes it also takes a great deal of practice to move past the desire to punch something—or someone. There are certainly times I wish God would stop putting certain people in my life to give me practice with this particular discipline."

We both laughed, but when I saw Reed come into the office later that afternoon, I knew that Grayson was being given one gigantic opportunity to practice.

REED

I WAS PISSED AFTER the deacons' meeting. I mean really pissed.

Everyone knew it, especially Grayson. You can imagine his surprise, but then, when I showed up at his office a few weeks later—all smiles.

"What can I do for you, Reed?" he asked, without getting up from his chair.

"I've been thinking, maybe it's time for a truce."

"A truce? Are we at war?" He leaned back in his chair causing it to creak. *That old chair is probably one of the last remnants of the church the way it used to be*, I thought. He stared at me, waiting for a response.

"Not war exactly," I finally said. "More like minor skirmishes." I tried to smile.

"I suppose you're right." He leaned forward, the chair creaking again. He looked down at the desk for a moment before looking back at me. "I never meant to pick a fight with you."

"Well, it takes two to fight," I said, but I had to swallow hard to stop the words I really wanted to say from tumbling out. Grayson was one of the few people I knew who could make me want to temporarily forget I'm a Christian. I guess it was all of the hurt people he left in his wake or maybe the way he was so dismissive of the church he came to serve—the church that never asked him to come in and transform it into some sort of self-help center with feel-good teachings. We were never in need of entertainers. We just wanted someone who was a willing vessel for the living fire of God. Of course anytime someone came close to saying such a thing to Grayson, he would ignore them, or worse yet, even roll his eyes when he thought no one was looking.

He didn't know, didn't want to know, why that church meant so much to me. It's in my blood, literally. My grandpa Williams was a charter member and he was convinced that the church rescued him from a dangerous path. To hear him tell it, he was a wild buck in his youth—drinking and cussing and fighting, usually over some girl, well one particular girl really. He'd see her often, coming out of the church near the pool hall. He and his pals had always laughed at the people coming in and out of that church, how uptight and straitlaced they were. They used to make sport of catcalling women just to watch them blush and rush inside. Grandpa never saw anything wrong with it until he saw her. She was a long-legged beauty with hair as black as a raven and eyes as green as honeydew—"a tall drink of water," he had told me, pointing to the black and white photograph of Grandma Williams he kept on the mantle.

Of course she wasn't like any of the girls he used to go with. She was quiet and refined, not the kind of girl that would normally give a punk like him the time of day. And she wouldn't have if he hadn't stopped his friends from catcalling her, even though they gave him a hard time about it. She started letting him walk her to the library or the school, but never to her home because of what her daddy would have done to him if he ever found out what kind of boy he was. And then one day she invited him to a tent revival that had come to town. He had no interest in religion really, but he had fallen in love with her, so he went. What he didn't figure on was falling in love with Jesus.

He wasn't expecting to be swept away by the rhythms of the skinny, hawk-nosed preacher, the kind of preacher he'd made fun of so many times. But there he was, hanging on every word, feeling the weight of his sin pressing down on him and knowing he couldn't live like that any longer. He knew it wasn't about getting right with the pretty girl sitting beside him anymore—although he was still plenty sweet on her. It was about getting right with God. As the service reached its fever pitch, he found himself rushing down the aisle and asking Jesus into his heart. They took him and the others that had come to salvation right down to the river to be baptized, and when he came up out of the water—his sins all washed away—and saw her smiling at him from the bank, he knew he was not only going to marry her but that together they were going to do great things in the name of the Lord. It was not long after my mother was born that they helped start the church, calling it New Hope Baptist Church because that's what Grandpa Williams said God had given him—new hope.

That church has been a part of every important family event ever since. Births, deaths, weddings, funerals, baptisms, ordinations. Just name it and you can bet New Hope had something to do with it. To see Grayson tear the church apart, to see him callously toss aside the very heart of it, was the same as if he had stomped all over their graves. So who could blame me that I jumped at the first chance I could find to get him out of that church. Certainly not most of the deacons. They understood, or at least I thought they did. But they backed down as soon as it got a little uncomfortable, leaving me the villain in Grayson's drama.

For days I was so mad that, without even realizing it, I was snapping at Sue. Finally she made me go fishing. I'm sure she was tired of the way I'd been treating her, through no fault of hers, but she knew that being on the lake calms my soul. You'd think that sitting alone for hours waiting for fish to bite would be irritating, but there's a serenity that comes from being on the water. And there's a satisfaction that comes from catching fish. It all comes from knowing what bait to use and finding the best fishing spot and then waiting. "You have to develop patience if you want to be a good fisherman," Dad once told me. "That's not a bad lesson to learn about life either," he added, patting me on the head.

I had forgotten that lesson with Grayson. I had tried to rush the process instead of figuring out the right bait and waiting for the right moment. I wasn't sure how long I'd have to wait, but I knew I needed to calm the waters. So I came to make peace with Grayson. As I watched him lean back in his chair and relax, I knew that I'd found the right lure. I just had to be patient enough to get him on the hook and reel him in.

BLESSED ARE THE MERCIFUL

HANK

IT WAS ALREADY GETTING dark outside even though the Mercy Savings and Loan sign showed it was just a little past five thirty and twenty-nine degrees. Twenty-nine frickin' degrees. Winter has never been my favorite time of the year. I hate the smothering darkness that makes nights seem endless. I hate the bitter cold—slept too many nights out there when I couldn't get warm. Actually when only a bottle of whiskey could make me feel warm, or at least not make me care if I was cold. *Maybe that's finally behind me*, I thought as I watched the headlights come and go in front of the church.

The diner was starting to get crowded. Too crowded for my comfort. If I hadn't already told the reverend to meet me there, I would have rushed outside, I don't care how cold it was. But I knew he was coming, or at least he said he'd be there. It was almost ten minutes past the time he said he'd meet me. Maybe I misunderstood. Maybe he finally decided he'd had enough of me and all my shit. I wouldn't have blamed him. I had fucked up my life and no matter how hard I tried...No, that's a lie. I never tried. Not even after two stints in county for drunk and disorderly. Not until the halfway house. Maybe that's been the only time in my life I tried. The reverend helped me get into it, the halfway house. I didn't want to go at first. Another ninety days in county detention would've suited me fine. At least it was warm and dry. But the reverend, he told me the halfway house was a chance to turn things around, not that I was convinced it was really possible. I didn't deserve a second chance, and I told him so.

"That, my friend," he said, "is what grace is all about. None of us deserves a second chance, but God gives it to us anyway. It's a gift. Take it."

I didn't trust gifts, and certainly not from God, but the reverend was pretty hard to say no to, so I went. The first few days were rough only because detox is always bad. The tremors and the nightmares are the worst. Flashes of killing or being killed filled my dreams and I'd wake up screaming. Or I'd wake up to one of the other guys in the house screaming, fighting off his own demons. There were ten of us in the house. We mostly kept to ourselves except when we were required to go to group meetings or eat meals. We couldn't afford to be weighted down with someone else's burden. I knew I could never inflict mine on anyone else. None of us were there to make friends anyway—just doing our time and getting out of there. During the day, we were either out looking for a job or working, which we were required to do. I found work at a factory cleaning toilets and mopping floors. Not the most glamourous job, and it would have felt good doing something outside myself for a change, except for the unsettling echo of basic training.

"Need a refill on your coffee?" the waitress asked—Ramie I think her name was. I nodded and she poured the coffee. "He'll be here, don't worry." I looked up at her and she smiled. "He's a man of his word."

"I've always known him to be." I smiled back at her. As she walked away, I thought about how different she was from the person who chased me from the dumpster out back or threatened to call the cops if I lingered too long in front of the diner. A lot can happen in ten years to change a person. But as I fought off the tremor that was making it impossible to stir my coffee, I knew that change doesn't come without a cost.

When the bank clock showed a quarter 'til six, I thought about giving up on waiting. The house had strict policies on coming and going and I had only received permission to be out until six thirty. It was a good ten-minute walk to the house from the diner. I was gathering my coat and gloves when I saw him rushing across the street and into the diner. He took off his hat and gloves and looked around before spotting me.

"Hey, man, I'm so sorry I'm late," he said when he sank onto the seat. "A call came in just as I was heading out the door. I tried to rush them off, but you know how it is." He looked exhausted and I wondered if it was right to burden him with more shit. But he looked at me so earnestly and said, "How are you doing, Hank?" It wasn't just a casual question, the kind you ask without really expecting—or wanting—an honest answer.

"I've been better, Rev. But I've also been worse. Fourteen days sober now."

He nodded. "It's a journey, isn't it?"

"To hell and back—at least I hope I'm on my way back." Ramie came to the table with the coffee and a menu. She and the reverend spoke to each other with such warmth and ease, and I was surprised by the envy swelling in me.

"It's been hard," I said after she left, "but I think I'm finally beginning to realize that I can't do this on my own."

"That's good, Hank. It's an important step, and the good news is that you don't have to do it alone."

"I know. I also know that I've hurt a lot of people and I need to make amends."

"I see that you're working the program."

"Trying to anyway. That's why I'm here tonight."

He looked puzzled. "Is there someone else coming?"

"No, I need to square something with you."

"Me? Look, Hank..." I put my hand up to stop him.

"Please. Let me just do this. It's been hard coming to terms with the things I've done in my life 'cause I've done some awful shitty things. But there's one thing that's been eating away at me for a long time now. Do you remember the time I stayed in the church, the night of the big storm?" He nodded. "Before I left that night, I took some money from your desk. I never stole from anyone before, you need to know that. And I wish like hell I hadn't then. So I wanted to say I'm sorry and I want to give this to you." I reached into my pocket and brought out a couple of fives and laid them on the table. "I don't remember exactly how much it was, but I think this is about right, with maybe a little interest on it."

He looked at the money on the table and I waited for him to pick it up. Instead, he looked up and me and smiled.

"I don't think you understand," I said as I nudged the money closer to him. "I said I stole this from you ten years ago."

"I know," he said, staring again at the money. "I saw that it was missing the next morning."

"But you never said anything about it. All these years…"

He didn't look up from the money. "'I will have mercy on whom I will have mercy,'" he said, his voice soft and almost distant, like he was talking to himself, "'and I will have compassion on whom I will have compassion.' It doesn't depend on human desire or effort, Hank, but on God's mercy." He looked at me, and I swear he looked like he might cry. "Grace and mercy are gifts. But like any good gift, they're useless if you won't accept them."

Dishes were clinking and people were talking all around us, but we were silent. I wanted a drink. In moments like this, when it became too painful to bear what I was feeling, I always wanted a drink. Now there was nothing left to numb it.

"I better get back to the house," I finally said.

"Let me drive you. It's too cold for you to walk."

I should have said no, but I was tired and weak. He left the money on the table when we got up to go. "Aren't you going to take the money?" I asked.

"Why don't we let it be someone else's gift now," he said as he patted me on the back and followed me out into the cold.

TYLER

By the time I was in my senior year of high school, my dad and I were distant planets—in the same galaxy but light years apart. Or so it seemed at times. We had established an uneasy truce, erupting into battle only a handful of times. To avoid the inevitable battle, we mostly resorted to mundane conversations like two strangers passing time on a long flight. It's not that either of us wanted it that way. I know I didn't. It would have been nice to have the easy going relationship that he had with Blake, and I was pretty sure Dad felt the same way about my relationship with Mom.

Maybe that's what prompted Dad to suggest a backpacking trip, just the two of us. Maybe, like me, he could recall the bond we shared sitting around the campfire telling ghost stories or singing songs while he played his guitar. For those moments around the campfire, he wasn't the Reverend Grayson Armstrong, full of righteous obligations. He was just Dad.

Sometimes I wondered what my life would have been like if he wasn't a pastor, though the pointless wondering did nothing except make my heart heavier.

As the day of the camping trip approached, we prepared for it as if we were preparing for a funeral, dragging out old memories with every piece of camping equipment, as if somehow sensing that those memories could not be recreated. Perhaps we both realized that this trip was the final elegy, a lament for what should have been. I suppose it was that realization that also brought with it a sense of dread.

We were both grateful to hit the trail, because the hour-long drive to get there was painfully quiet. But something about stepping into the dense woods breathed life into us both. We teased each other about whose pack was lighter and soaked in the majestic autumn view from a ridgeline. Hope for restoration seemed less doomed to failure.

A couple of hours before nightfall, we found a clearing by a stream and made camp. Dad pitched the tents while I gathered firewood. When I came back with an armload of twigs, Dad was softly singing "Shall We Gather at the River." He smiled at me as if I'd caught him swearing, like I'd done when I was a little boy. "Being down by a creek always makes me think of your Grandpa Armstrong," he said. I nodded, though it was curious that Dad would be thinking of Grandpa in such a pleasant way. He had always described his father as strict and unyielding.

After eating dinner and tying the food pack up in a nearby tree, we huddled around the fire as the night air grew colder. We were quiet for a while, listening to the fire crackle and the crickets chirp nearby. I didn't often sense God in a church building, but out among the trees, whose leaves rustled above me, I sensed his presence. I thought about the image of him as the father, an image I had been taught all my life. I could never figure out if God was a loving, benevolent father or a harsh, foreboding one. I guess the answer depended on who was required to respond.

"Did you love your father?" I said, barely above a whisper.

Dad didn't answer right away, sensing, I guess, the root of the question.

"Yes," he said, "Despite everything, I did."

"Do you think I love you—despite everything?"

"I'd like to think so." His voice was soft, full of regret.

We let the thought settle along with the cold air that hung close to the ground. I picked up a twig and held it in the flames until the end caught fire, and then I pulled it out and watched the tiny flame struggle on its own. All during high school, I had been that tiny flame—struggling, but at least not entirely on my own. Rachel had kept me from completely giving up.

She told me life would get better once I was in college—to keep hanging on, so I did. I never told her everything that happened with Kevin, but she knew it was bad. She also knew that Kevin tormented me until he was sent off to an alternative school. He never told anyone about the night at his cousin's house, at least not that I could tell. Instead, he seemed to take greater pleasure in personally teasing me than in ceding that pleasure to anyone else. When no one else was looking, he'd pucker his lips, or if he was really trying to needle me, he'd thrust his hips in an obscene motion. Even Rachel didn't know how bad it was, though she tried to get me to talk to the guidance counselor. I knew that would make things worse. If I believed in hell, I imagined it would be filled with *Kevin's*.

I looked up at Dad and he was staring at me. His face was a play of light and shadow from the fire, giving it an ominous distortion.

"You know I love you, don't you?" he said.

I looked back at the twig in my hand. The flame had gone out.

"Even if I'm gay," I said, not looking back at him, sensing the answer that was coming. My mind—my soul—braced for it. *I wish the flames would just consume me as they do the dead branches*, I thought as I waited for his answer.

"Of course, but—" He stopped himself, perhaps because he realized that there shouldn't have been any conditions on the statement or perhaps because he was embarrassed about it being a conditional response. "I don't think you know your own mind yet," he finally said.

"Are you saying that because you're terrified I *am* gay?"

"I'm saying it because you're seventeen. You're too young to really know what you want."

"That's a cop out, Dad. Can't you just admit that you don't want me to be gay?"

"Please don't put words in my mouth. I don't want you to be unhappy, that's all."

"I've been unhappy for a long time, but that didn't seem to bother you—until now. Now that you know the truth." I looked at him, daring him to say it wasn't so.

"I think maybe we should stop this conversation before we say things we'll regret."

I wanted to scream at him that he was a coward, but he stood up. "It's getting late. I'm going to turn in." He came over and patted my head like I was still six and he was consoling me after losing the t-ball game. A part of me longed for those days, when he could give me a pat and, with a few words and a kind smile, make everything okay again. But we were both different people by then. Years of battle scars had changed us both. "See you in the morning," he said.

After he crawled into his tent and zipped it up, I focused on the embers, glowing bright red, particularly a small clump that had fallen away from the flames. Without flames to feed them, they would likely be the first to grow cold. Instinctively, I poured the last bit of water in my cup over them to help them die more quickly, and then I headed to my tent and closed myself inside, shutting out everything but the sound of the trees bending to the wind.

BRYSON

P.T. Barnum supposedly said "there's a sucker born every minute." Sometimes I think he had Grayson in mind when he said it. Grayson was a soft touch, a sucker for any sob story he heard. The church gave him a small allowance for benevolence—you know, the occasional person who seeks out churches to get necessities, such as food and diapers, or help with rent or utilities or gas. It was not uncommon for Grayson to use up the benevolence fund within a short time. But he'd still give people money from his own pocket. "Natalie tells me I'm not allowed to carry my wallet anymore," he often joked. I bet it wasn't too far from the truth.

One time I was with him when a couple came into the church looking for a handout. They looked shady to me. They had that Bohemian hippy-chick look, and I bet they hadn't bathed in a week, probably longer. A little girl with them was toddling around with her dirty bare feet and a smudge of dirt on her face. The man said they were passing through town when their van broke down. He had spent all day trying to get the part that they needed, which they finally got. But the part cost them every dime they had, so they hadn't eaten all day. Grayson got them some food from the church's food bank. He even brought a big cookie for the girl, who promptly plopped on the floor and began eating it, with crumbs falling all around her.

Grayson talked to the couple for a while. The man claimed he had a job waiting down south so that's where they were headed. I watched Grayson as he took in every word. While little flags were going up in my mind, he seemed to accept the story without question. And then, when they thanked him for the food and said they would be getting on the road, he asked them if they had a place to stay for the night. They were just going to sleep in the van, the man said, looking all pitiful. He played that well, because of course Grayson wasn't going to let that happen. He followed them to a motel next to the interstate, with me in tow, and paid for a room for them for the night. While I waited for Grayson to get them checked in, I saw a dog in their beat up van. *They can't afford food for themselves, but they have a dog?* I wondered.

I mentioned that to Grayson when he got back into the car. "I bet you paid for that out of your own pocket. You know, they just took you for a ride," I said to him.

"Maybe," he replied. "But my job isn't to judge them or their circumstances. I'm called—we're all called—to help those in need. God will sort the rest out later."

I nodded. I mean, what else could I do? But to myself, I was shaking my head. Yeah, Barnum would have had a field day with Grayson.

NATALIE

It might have killed our marriage, and even though it didn't, it left a gaping wound for a while. *I haven't been completely honest with you.* His words echoed on the wind as I mindlessly forced the porch swing to rock back and forth. The cool night air washed over me, stinging my face as it dried my tears, while the slow, steady rhythm of the clinking chains above me played counterpoint to my rapidly beating heart. I should have never listened to Effie. I told her it was only gossip.

"I didn't say I believed it, honey," she said as she patted my hand. "I just thought you needed to know that the rumor was out there."

I love Effie like a second mother, but I wanted to say to her, no, I don't need to know this. The things people said to my face about Grayson were bad enough, but the very idea that Grayson was having an affair was ridiculous.

"I know, dear. I wouldn't have given it any credence at all except that he does spend a lot of time over at that diner, and someone also saw them together at the park the other day."

"So you *do* think there's a possibility it's true?" My heart began to race.

"Of course not." She grabbed my hand and gave it a firm squeeze. "Grayson would never do such a thing. He loves you and the children too much for that. I just meant that I can see where some people might misread his actions."

"Well, that's their problem not ours," I said as I crossed my arms to signal that I was finished talking about the matter. She got the hint and moved on to another topic, but I couldn't really say what it was. My mind kept wandering back to that diner and flashing every image I could conjure of that woman. In all the years we had been in Mercy, I had only been in the diner a couple of times. Grayson had introduced me to her once, but I had long since forgotten her name. Her face, though—her face was hanging in my memory. The brownish blond bangs on either side of her forehead that just touched the top of her full eyebrows. The rounded, flat nose dotted with light freckles, making her look younger than she probably was. Her full, pale lips set firm—reflecting determination rather than anger, I think. Perhaps it was her eyes, though, that stayed with me the most. The dark brown eyes were those of a wounded animal, fear overwhelming an unspeakable sadness. And though I doubted there was anything to the rumor, I could see why Grayse might be drawn to her. His instinct was to protect the wounded.

I watched him at dinner that night. If he had heard the rumors, he certainly didn't show it. He joked with Blake, like he always did, and all the while carried on a silly conversation with Hannah. Every once in a while, he'd look over at me and smile. An innocent "I'm not guilty of anything" smile. I forced one in return. Not because I thought he was guilty but because I felt guilty for even entertaining the thought that he might be.

When we crawled into bed that night, I snuggled close to him—close enough to catch the faint scent of his aftershave. It was a comforting smell. Familiar. A reminder that my life was not full of shadows and mysteries or clandestine trysts.

Our marriage was a fortress—a place to protect love not just keep intruders out. Very little had been able to penetrate its walls over the years, so maybe I had become complacent. Maybe we both had. Maybe that's why I couldn't shake the doubt that was opening a crack in the fortress wall drip by drip.

A week went by before I finally decided to speak to Grayse about it. He was out back on the porch swing lightly strumming his guitar. The sound of the faint melody was the only way I knew he was there because the only light was on the other side of the porch coming through the kitchen window.

"Is Hannah asleep?" he asked while continuing to play softly.

"I think so, but she's pretty restless. I doubt we've seen the last of her tonight."

"Poor thing. She certainly wasn't feeling well at dinner. I think she misses her brothers."

"I know," I said as I sat on the swing beside him. A slight chill was settling in, as it often does on spring evenings. I pulled my sweater tighter and let the silence hang between us as he continued to play.

"I need to ask you something," I finally said.

"Sure. Am I in trouble again?" He laughed, trying to make light of it, but when I didn't respond he laid the guitar against the wall and leaned back in the swing. "This sounds serious," he said.

"I guess that depends on your answer." I cleared my throat. I had not anticipated how hard it really would be to talk about it. "Apparently people have been talking..."

He relaxed a bit. "People are always talking, Nat," he said.

"I know. Normally I don't pay any attention to the chatter, but this time—"

"What's different about this time?"

"This time it's about you and another woman."

"Another woman?" I could hear a tremor in his voice. "Surely you don't believe I'd ever—"

"I didn't believe it. I don't want to believe it."

"But?"

I couldn't explain to him that I trusted him—had always trusted him—yet in spite of that I let doubt creep in like a thief to steal that trust. I couldn't tell him that I'd gone to the diner to see her. Not that seeing her answered any questions or erased the nagging doubt. That in spite of my shame for doubting him, I needed confirmation from him that it wasn't true. "But I need to hear it from you," I finally said.

"That I'm not having an affair?" He reached over in the darkness and grabbed my hand. "No," he said emphatically. "No, I'm not having an affair and I've never had an affair. I wouldn't do that and I won't ever do that." I exhaled, not realizing that I had been holding my breath. "But I haven't been completely honest with you."

"What?" I said, trying to jerk my hand loose. But he held onto it.

"I haven't been totally honest," he repeated. He was quiet for a while but still gripped my hand, like he was afraid if he let go I would disappear into the night. A couple of times it seemed as if he was about to speak only to let the moment slip by. Finally, he pulled his hand away and stood up, making the chains clink. He walked to the other side of the deck.

"Just say it for God's sake," I said, the dread welling up in me.

"This is harder than I thought it would be." He paused again and the silence widened the gap between us. Finally, his words came, tentative and careful. "It's true that I haven't had an affair, but I have to admit that I've thought about it before."

"Thought about it?" I blinked back tears.

"It was a long time ago, when the boys were young—before we came to Mercy." He was silhouetted against the light coming from the kitchen. It was hard not being able to see his face, to read his emotions, which I had learned to do fairly well over the years. But this silhouetted form was unfamiliar and strange. At that moment he was a stranger to me. "I was feeling left out," he continued. "You were busy taking care of the boys and had your hands full. I was too young and immature to fully understand what that meant or that my lack of help had anything to do with it. All I knew was that I was lonely."

I tried to focus on the shape in front of me, to transform it back into the Grayson I knew. I realized after we married that he was not as mature as I had first thought but more surprisingly, he was not as confident and self-assured as he had seemed. I sensed that same awkward boy had returned.

"It was just harmless flirting," the disembodied voice said. "But I lost myself in the attention. She made me feel special—"

"And I didn't," I said, my voice betraying the hurt.

"I didn't think so at the time. Sometimes it felt like you only had time for the boys, which meant that you were too tired to do anything with me. And you seemed so angry with me all the time."

"So it's my fault that you thought about having an affair?"

"No, of course not. I was an idiot—and selfish. Of course I

didn't see it that way back then." He returned to the swing and sat down. He searched for my hand with a frantic urgency. "Nothing came of it, Nat. I swear," he said when he finally found it. He drew my hand to his chest.

"So why are you telling me this now?"

"I don't know. I guess lately I've just been thinking about how much the past can be a burden on the present, especially if you try to bury it."

"So it has nothing to do with any guilt you have about the woman at the diner."

"The diner? You mean Ramie?" He paused to let it sink in. "So that's what has people talking?"

"Yes," I whispered.

He sighed. "It has nothing to do with her, at least not in the way they think. I've watched her over the years be weighted down by her past—by the terrible things that have happened to her. She's been adrift for quite some time and I've just been trying to shine a light to guide her back to shore."

I started to respond, but a tiny voice interrupted us. Hannah stood at the screen door trying to peer outside.

"Daddy?"

"I'm here, pumpkin. What do you need?"

"Can I get a drink of water?"

"Sure." Before he stood up, he squeezed my hand. "Are we okay?" he asked.

"We will be," I said softly.

He hoisted Hannah on his shoulders when he got to the door, and then disappeared inside. I stayed on the swing for a while, listening to the clinking chains above me and the faint little-girl giggles from somewhere in the house. I believed Grayson, yet the tears came because I knew in my heart that he had a mistress. One who called to Grayson from a rocky shore to have him save others who had crashed there. I knew that even I could not drown out her seductive song.

GLADYS

I SEEN THEM AT the park, Ramie and that preacher. Ramie always talks about him. I've known Ramie for years, ever since I worked at the diner with her before I got my disability, but I just wanted to tell her to shut up already. It's always Grayson this and Grayson that. He's a nice man, and handsome. Can't say that I didn't have my own fantasies when he come into the diner all the time. He would have never been interested in women like us anyway.

Ramie told me that there was nothing to it because he was married. But that's never stopped her before, and I seen them all cozied up on that park bench. He was holding her hands and staring into her eyes. "You're playing with fire," I told her. She just told me to mind my own business. So I told her "Fine." I didn't talk to her no more about it, if she was going to be that way, but I know what I seen and I knowed someone was going to get burned and burned bad.

EFFIE

It wasn't like I was trying to stir up trouble between Natalie and Grayson. They were not only friends, but they were also like my own children. But I was worried, for both of them. I had heard the talk for a while and basically dismissed it, just because I knew Grayson well enough to believe it was not true.

Fred and I had talked about it often enough, though. Grayson took too many risks. Even when he was reminded, as he often was by Fred, that his actions could be misunderstood and have unintended consequences, he'd just brush it off. "The only one whose opinion matters is the one who asked me to take care of the least of these. I'd rather disappoint busybodies than disobey him," he said. Of course we couldn't argue with that, which made it all the more frustrating. How could Grayson be so naive to think that people wouldn't talk, or do something even worse?

So I went to Natalie hoping maybe she'd understand the gravity of it all, even if Grayson didn't. Maybe she'd have better luck getting him to rethink some of his risky behavior. I certainly didn't expect her to react the way she did, though in hindsight I'm not sure why I didn't expect it.

"Effie, I'm surprised you're telling me this," she said. "That's just malicious gossip." Her mouth was tight, indignant really, but her eyes betrayed her fear.

"I didn't say I believed it, honey," I said. I patted her hand, trying to ease her mind. "I wouldn't have thought anything at all about it but he does spend a lot of time over at that diner. Someone even saw them in the park together the other day." I couldn't bear to tell her it was me—and that it seemed cozier than it should have been.

"So you *do* think there's a possibility it's true?" Her eyes were as big as saucers.

"Of course not. Grayson loves you and the children too much to do such a thing. I just thought you needed to know that the rumor was out there. Sometimes I worry that people might misunderstand his actions."

She crossed her arms, like she was pouting. "Well, that's their problem," she said. I knew better than to keep talking about it. She could be as stubborn as Grayson. When I told Fred about her reaction, he said he wasn't surprised.

"Maybe you could talk to Grayson," I said.

"Absolutely not." He put his arm around me and squeezed. "I know you mean well, Effie, but we need to stay out of this."

I nodded. He was probably right, and I was prepared to let it drop even though I worried it might be a mistake. If people in the church had been talking, and truly began believing something was going on, it could mean the end of Grayson at the church. Even if he didn't seem to care what others had to say, I couldn't bear the thought of him and Natalie leaving. So I bided my time. In spite of what Fred thought, if the opportunity seemed right I was determined to talk to Grayson about it.

Most days when I arrived at the office he was already there. If his door was open, he'd call out 'good morning' in a way that reminded me of when I taught kindergarten. But I noticed a change in his mood about a week after I talked to Natalie. They must have talked afterward, because he began brooding about the office. He got that way every now and then, so I didn't think much of it at first, even when he was barely speaking to me. After a few days of this, though, I finally decided that maybe the opportunity I'd been waiting for was presenting itself.

"Do you have a minute?" I said as I lightly tapped on his open door. He looked up from the book he was reading and motioned for me to sit. "We've been friends for a long time," I said after I sat down across from him. He nodded, but waited for me to continue. "So I know when something's bothering you." I paused, giving him the invitation to talk.

As he stared at me, his blue eyes narrowed a bit as he considered whether to say anything. "I understand you talked to Natalie about some rumor involving me," he finally said.

"Yes," I replied, finally realizing what was behind his mood.

"For God's sake, Effie, why?" His voice was tinged with anger, but I also heard the desperation. "Didn't you stop to consider what that would do to her, not to mention to our marriage?"

"Your marriage?"

He saw the panic on my face. "We're fine," he said in response. He looked past me, as if he was replaying whatever had happened between them. "I just don't understand why you would do that to her—to us."

"I didn't mean to hurt either of you. I hope you believe that. I care too much for both of you to do that intentionally."

"I know," he said. He grew quiet. His fingers were tightly laced, as if they had been knitted together, but his thumbs were in constant motion as they twirled around each other. He was wrestling with something. So was I.

"Are you mad at me?" I finally said.

"Not mad. Just disappointed." He moved his hands to his mouth as if in a posture for prayer. "You were someone I thought I could trust," he said softly.

He probably couldn't have said anything more painful to me than that. The words hurt me in much the same way my words to Natalie must have hurt him. I looked at his face, which, despite the passage of more than a decade, looked as youthful as when I first met him. Yet, faint lines had begun to form on his forehead, giving witness to the years of struggle at the church, even as it had grown and flourished. But a successful, vibrant church didn't stop the naysayers from grumbling. To know that I was even an unintentional part of that, at least in his eyes, broke my heart.

"Maybe it would be a good idea for you to find someone else to work in the office," I said. "Someone you can trust." My voice cracked as I held back tears. He stared blankly at me, fighting back his own tears, I think. I rose from my chair and walked to my desk, pausing only for a moment when I got to his office door.

I yanked my purse out of the desk drawer, tucked it under my arm, and headed to my car. It wasn't until I pulled into the driveway at home that I allowed the tears to come, tears that had no doubt been gathering for many years.

FRED

Effie surprised me when she came home from the church well before her usual quitting time. So I would have known something was wrong even if I hadn't seen her red, puffy eyes. She wasn't one who was prone to crying, which I was grateful for. There's nothing harder to deal with than a woman's tears—at least nothing to make a man feel more helpless.

She didn't say anything at first—didn't try to explain the tears—choosing instead to grab her gardening gloves and head to the flower bed out front. Tending to the flowers had always been her therapy. I knew she would share with me what was going on when she was ready, so I let her be alone for a while. I watched her from the window as she gently freed the flowers from the greedy weeds, showing the same tenderness she had shown to countless little children over the years.

After a few minutes, I joined her outside. "Need some help?" I said as I eased down onto the ground beside her. She said nothing but when she looked at me and smiled I was glad I was sitting down. Even after more than fifty years together, her smile could still take my breath away. We worked in silence for a while. Every now and then I glanced in her direction, waiting for a signal that she was ready to talk.

"I quit my job today," she finally said, not looking up from the flowers.

"That's rather sudden," I said, trying not to let the shock register in my voice. She loved her job, but she loved Grayson even more. "Did something happen?"

"I messed up." Her voice faltered. She turned to me, tears slipping down her cheeks. "Oh, Fred, I hurt him by going to Natalie. I didn't mean to. You know I didn't."

"I know, and I suspect Grayson knows it, too."

"If you could have seen his face. It was worse than when he's dealing with Reed." We each paused on those words since we knew how much Grayson bristled at everything Reed had done to him and to the church by planting seeds of discontent and then gleefully watering them with half-truths until people finally left. "I just couldn't bear it if Grayson thought I would do something to hurt him intentionally," Effie finally said.

"Did he actually say that?"

"Not in so many words. But he must wonder. After everything he's been through, he must wonder if I've turned on him like so many others have. I'm not sure it will ever be the same between us."

"Maybe I should have talked to him like you suggested. Do you want me to talk to him about your job?" I wasn't exactly keen on the idea, but if Effie had felt the need to quit I wondered if maybe she had misunderstood Grayson's feelings.

"Please don't," she said as she grabbed my arm, like I was going to jump up immediately and go find Grayson. I put my hand over hers to reassure her. Even through the thick gardening glove, I could feel it trembling.

"We'll let it be, then," I said. I had rarely confronted Grayson anyway, had rarely seen the need to. Maybe I had too easily dismissed the concerns of others. Maybe I had been too quick to excuse Grayson's behavior. *Should we leave the church*, I wondered. *Should I tell Grayson why, if we did decide to leave*? As I wondered what to do next, I was struck with the irony that normally I would have asked myself what Grayson would do in such a situation, would probably have talked it over with him. I was still trying to figure it out when Sunday came around.

Effie decided to stay home, not that I blamed her. She sent me on, though. "It just wouldn't feel right if neither of us there," she said. It didn't really make sense to me, but it seemed important to her. So I went.

The second service of the morning was just starting when I arrived at the church. A few people from the first service still lingered by the coffee station and others were chatting in a small clump while trying occasionally to snag one of their children who were content to be chasing each other in the wide open space. I nodded a hello before ducking into the dimly lit worship center. After my eyes adjusted to the darkness, I saw that everyone was on their feet singing. I found an empty seat on the back row and slid past three or four people to get to it.

The music was loud, so much so that the stage lights and even my own heart seemed to pulse to the rhythm of the drum. Everything in the room felt connected—woven together into a single fabric. But there were loose threads hidden underneath that threatened to expose holes if tugged too much. There were certainly many who had tried over the years, but now I wondered if Effie and I had tugged on one of those threads. Were we about to open a gaping hole?

When Grayson took the stage, he flashed the smile that welcomed sinners but sometimes frustrated saints. People like Reed saw it as self-righteous, even phony. Maybe it was. Maybe every pastor has a phony smile, one they learned in some course at seminary, to hide their self-doubts. Grayson wasn't immune to those doubts. But he knew doubt was usually seen as occupational suicide. As spiritual leaders, ministers weren't supposed to have doubt—any kind of doubt. To many people, doubt is the absence of faith. At one time I believed that was true, until I met Grayson.

He had been at the church maybe three years the first time we talked about it. I had stopped by the church in the middle of the afternoon to talk over the plans for a food bank at the church. When he wasn't in his office, I went looking for him. I found him in the sanctuary—we had not yet built the worship center. He was kneeling at the stage, with his forehead resting against it. It took me a while to get used to having a stage instead of an altar. Grayson had defended the decision—his decision—to transform the sanctuary into a more contemporary worship space. To Grayson the stage was just as much of an altar, and I had certainly backed him over the likes of Reed. But I had to admit that it never did feel the same. Yet there was Grayson, on his knees in front of it. I debated turning around and leaving him to his prayers. It didn't matter, though, because while I was wrestling with the decision, Grayson looked up and saw me.

"I'm sorry. I didn't mean to interrupt your prayer."

"It's all right. I've been struggling to stay focused today anyway. Sometimes God just seems so far away." He rose from his knees only to sit on the edge of the stage. I was startled by his admission. Preachers weren't supposed to feel distant from God, much less say it out loud. But Grayson had changed the way I thought about pastors. He had changed the way I thought about a lot of things, including religion.

Since the pews had been long gone, I grabbed a chair out of the front row and set it right in front of Grayson. "What's Reed done now?" I joked as I sat down.

"I wish that's all it was." He laughed, but the smile left his face almost as quickly as it had come. He stared at the floor. "Sometimes I wonder why God called me to the ministry. Sometimes I wonder if he even called me at all." He looked at me to measure the depth of my shock before he continued. "I got the call—or what I thought was the call—when I was in college, not long before I met Natalie. It was strange, actually. I had fallen away from the church and from God, mostly because it represented everything that I detested about my father."

He looked away again. "It was in my freshman year of college that I met my roommate's sister. We hit it off right away, even though she was a couple of years older than me. We dated for over a year, and it got pretty serious. But then she told me she was pregnant." He stood up and walked a few feet away, like he couldn't risk seeing my reaction. "She said she didn't want a baby," he continued. "At least not at that point in her life. When she told me she'd decided to get an abortion, I was so relieved that I didn't see the suffering in her eyes. All I could think of was that I wasn't ready to be a father at nineteen. I didn't try to talk her out of it." He came back and sat down again, pressing his hands so hard on the stage that it thrust his shoulders upward. "But what I'm most ashamed of was that I didn't even offer to go with her to the clinic. She told me how frightening it was to walk past people who were shouting insults. I could see in her eyes that she blamed me for making her do that alone, and she was right to do so."

I could see the weight of it still tormenting him. "People can make selfish mistakes when they're young," I said, trying to help make the burden lighter.

"It was a dark time for me," he continued. "I even thought about ending it all. But one night I was sitting in my dorm room and I found my old Bible tucked among my books. I opened it, which I hadn't done in quite some time, and it opened right to Psalm 147. I read the words, but it was like God was speaking right to me. *He heals the brokenhearted and binds up their wounds. He determines the number of the stars and calls them each by name. Great is our Lord and mighty in power; his understanding has no limit.* I took out my highlighter and marked the passage because I knew that was not only meant for me personally but it was meant for me to share with others."

"That seems a pretty clear calling to me."

"I suppose. But sometimes I feel like such a fraud. I mean, I'm the last person who should be telling people how to live their lives."

"So you're a flawed human being," I said. "As I recall, God tends to use flawed people to his glory."

"You're right, of course. Some days, though, it's easy to forget that. Some days I can't shake the awful things from my past and I find myself wondering why God even fools with me."

"He fools with you because he has given you a chance for redemption. He's given you his heart for people who need to find that same redemption."

"Thanks, Fred." We stood and hugged. "You're such a good friend. I'm grateful God brought you into my life."

I thought about that moment as I watched Grayson on the stage. Despite his occasional doubts—and mine—he had been anointed by God for this purpose. As he spoke of forgiveness and peace, I knew the words were meant for him as much as the person near me, who was sniffling. They were meant for me as well. I knew I couldn't confront Grayson, and even if Effie and I couldn't stay at the church, we wouldn't make some big scene, as Reed had done. Grayson didn't deserve that.

RAMIE

I PICKED UP THE old guitar and laid it across my lap. My fingers traced the smooth edges of the body and then down the long neck. I swear I could still feel the warmth of Daddy's hand as I wrapped my own around the neck and pressed my fingers against the frets. He was there. I felt him, like I always did when I held his guitar. I closed my eyes and listened for his voice. Most nights it came to me—softly, as if on the wind, I could hear the familiar sound of it and then my fingers would bring to life the melody. Would bring Daddy to life.

I could see him, sitting there on that worn out couch, the guitar perched on his knee. I could see me sitting on the floor at his feet, lost in the movement of his fingers on the strings and in the deep sound of his voice. Sometimes, before I could stop it, I could see Mommy, too, sitting beside him, her arm resting on his shoulder as she leaned into him. He loved her with his eyes as he sang to her and I knew I wanted someone to love me like that one day. He did love her. In spite of everything, he still loved her long after she was gone. I wished I could love her again, for his sake if not for mine.

It certainly wasn't for Jim's sake. He called a couple of months after Daddy passed. I wouldn't have ever answered the phone, except it was a number I didn't recognize.

"Hello, Ramie. This is Jim."

"Jim? Jim who?"

"Jim Reynolds. I used to be the pastor of Zion Revival Tabernacle." He couldn't bring himself to say the rest of it—that he was the one who broke a little girl's heart and sent a good man to an early grave. "We heard about your father, honey. Your mother and I were so sorry to hear it." I wanted to bless him out, or at the very least hang up. But I didn't. I couldn't, though I'm not sure why. Instead, I managed a "thank you" but said nothing else. "I want you to know," he continued, "that you still have a dad right here. If you ever need anything, I want you to call on me and your mother. You know, she sure would love it if you would call her or least write her back. She misses you," he said, not recognizing the absurdity of his statement. "She's real sorry for what she did, honey."

"Listen, Jim, I don't know how the hell you got my number, but don't call it again." I hung up before he could say anything more. After what he did to me and Daddy, he had some nerve to think that I could accept him as even a second-rate father, not to mention suggesting that I have anything to do with my mother. The last contact I'd had from her—that I accepted anyway—was the letter Mommy sent to me and Daddy a few months after she left. She was sorry, she wrote. She didn't mean to hurt anyone, but she had to do it. Mommy was miserable and she knew she was making everyone else miserable. She truly believed everyone would be happier this way.

Perhaps she was right about me being happier with her gone, but she was dead wrong about Daddy. No matter how he felt about her, though, we both knew that there wasn't any point in responding to the letter—or responding to any other attempt she made to contact us over the years, including using her own mother. I told Granny Whitson that Mommy had made her bed and I was going to make sure it was a cold day in hell before she ever got out of it.

That was before I got the letter from Naomi, Mommy and Brother Reynolds' youngest child. The envelope, which I hadn't opened, lay on the coffee table in front of me as I strummed the guitar. I stared at the big block letters on the bottom of the envelope that said PLEASE READ followed by three exclamation marks. I had been tempted to throw the letter in the trash, like I had done with all the letters and cards I'd gotten from my mother or her new family. But something in the urgency of the message on the front made me keep it. Keeping it and reading it were two different things, though, and I was not at all sure that I was ready for whatever Naomi had to say.

I don't know what I expected. They were all strangers to me—Naomi and her brothers. Even Mommy was a stranger by that time. The woman I knew only came in flashes of memory. Like the way her long dark hair tickled me as a I nestled against her perfumed neck. The way her nose crinkled when she laughed. The way her voice fit perfectly with Daddy's when they sang together. But those memories were like a coral reef that had been damaged by exposure to toxins. They were in danger of extinction. Trying to resurrect those memories wasn't going to change what was in the letter or the hate that was anchored in my heart.

But the envelope pleaded with me to read its contents and Grayson had encouraged me to do it, so I laid my guitar on the coffee table. I picked up the envelope and studied my name in the delicate cursive and the postmark from somewhere in Tennessee. I flipped it over and ripped open the flap. A photograph fluttered to the floor when I unfolded the lavender stationary. I left it where it landed and began to read the letter.

Dear Sister,

I hope it's OK to call you that. Even though we've never met, I've always found it comforting to know I had a big sister out there, and I need comfort right now. There's no easy way to say this, so I'll just say it. Our mother is dying. The doctor says she may have only a few weeks left. She keeps asking about you, Ramie, and I don't know what to say to her. I know it's probably not right to do this, but I'm begging you to come see her. I'm not saying forgive her. Just let her see you one more time before she goes. She needs you and I really need my sister right now.

Please come. Please.

Love,

Naomi

The words floated in my mind for a while before settling back into a heap on the page I held in my hand. The weight of each word pounded over and over until I screamed and closed my fists, crumpling the letter into a little ball. I threw it across the room and bowed my head into my hands, waiting for the tears that should have come. But then my eyes found hers, staring up at me from the photograph that had fallen to the floor. Her face had changed, had become plumper. Lines were beginning to form on her forehead and her hair was streaked with gray, but her eyes were still as intense as I remembered. As I stared at her, anger swirled into longing and back to anger until I had to look away from her. That's when I really focused on the girl standing beside her. She was young, maybe fifteen or sixteen, and had long red hair. It had to be Naomi.

I studied her. The red hair and long, sharp nose must have been from her daddy, but her sweet smile was definitely Mommy's. A wave of envy washed over me as I stared at the two of them, arms linked and so happy. I hated them, and I hated myself for hating them. *Hate is such a destructive emotion.* Grayson's words echoed in my head.

I hadn't seen Grayson for a few weeks, so seeing him at the park a couple of days after Naomi's letter arrived was exactly what I needed. He had a way of showing up at just the right time. I was sitting on a bench near the back of the park trying to sort through the jumble of emotions stirred up by the letter. It seemed as if every time I was beginning to feel at peace with my life, I'd get some kind of contact from my mother or someone in her family, though I'd never heard from Naomi before. I wouldn't have even known Naomi existed if Granny Whitson wasn't constantly trying to tell me all about Mommy's new family. I tried to tell her that I didn't give a damn, but she'd rattle on about them anyway.

After I'd been stewing on that park bench for a while, I noticed a handsome man jogging on the path and heading in my direction. When he got closer, I realized it was Grayson. Sometimes I wished that he wasn't married or that he was the kind of man that didn't care if he was married, which seemed like the only kind of men who were ever attracted to me. But Grayson wasn't like that and no amount of fantasizing was going to change it.

"I thought that was you," he said as he stopped in front of me. His broad shoulders and toned arms glistened with sweat. "You looked so deep in thought that I figured it would be rude to interrupt you, but then I worried that not stopping would be rude, too. So what's a preacher to do?" We laughed because that question had been a joke between us for years. And then he got serious. "Do you need to talk or would you rather be alone?"

I signaled for him to have a seat. "Are you sure you have the time?" I asked. "I don't want to hold you up." I said it even though I knew what his answer was going to be. Grayson never hesitated to drop everything when someone appeared to need help or a shoulder to cry on—and the whole time he was with that person, he never checked his watch or phone, like he really had better things to do. He was always in the moment.

"It's my family," I said after he sat down. "Well, my mother's family. But what else is new, right?" He nodded. We'd had that conversation too many times before. "Anyway, I got a letter a couple of days ago from my stepsister."

"So what did it say that's got you so upset?"

"That's just it. I haven't even opened it." He looked puzzled, so I answered his unasked question. "I can't bring myself to read anything Mom sends or that she sends through her family. I usually throw them in the trash as soon as I get them."

"Why keep this one then?"

"I don't know. Partly, I guess, because she wrote 'please read' in big letters on the front. Mostly, though, there was something about the pleading on the front that felt familiar, that seemed reminiscent of the desperation I felt at that age."

"Well that's a place to start healing, don't you think?"

"I can't. I just can't," I protested. "Whatever connection I might feel toward her can't overcome the fact that she grew up with the mother I never had—that I should have had. It's not her fault, I know, but I still hate her for it. I hate all of them." I heard how it sounded coming out of my mouth and instantly felt ashamed. But Grayson's face showed no signs of judgment.

"Hate is such a destructive emotion, Ramie." It wasn't a criticism. I could see it in his eyes. "You think it hurts the people you hate—and sometimes it does—but trust me, hate ends up destroying you instead." He took my hand and stared at me with those penetrating eyes. "Maybe, just maybe, by connecting with this girl, you can begin to let grace and mercy guide your relationship with your mother."

"But that's like saying that what Mommy did was okay."

"No, what it's saying is that you've found enough peace that, despite what she's done, you can give her what she doesn't deserve—love and forgiveness."

I shook my head. "There's not enough peace in the whole world for that to happen."

"Then don't start by focusing on your mother. Focus on your stepsister instead. You said that there may be an echo of you in her. Why don't you start by reading her letter and just see where it takes you." We both stood and he wrapped his arms around me before stepping back and placing his hands on my shoulders. He made sure our eyes were locked before he added, "I have faith in you, Ramie."

I still felt his hug as I stared at Naomi's picture. Despite his faith in me, what he was asking me to do seemed impossible. Hate was rooted so deep that I didn't know if I had the strength to dig it out. But without even realizing it, mercy and grace had already begun to seep down and water a seed that Grayson had planted years ago. When I looked at Naomi again and saw her smile, the smile we both shared with Mommy, I knew what I had to do. I tucked the picture in my shirt pocket before going to the closet and grabbing my suitcase from the top shelf.

REED

The atmosphere under that big white tent was electric. Hundreds of people had come from all over the county—even some from other nearby counties—to hear the slate of preachers and choirs that had descended on Mercy for the big revival. I hadn't really seen anything like it since I was a child and went with my mother and Miss Addie to the one in Elmer. As frightening as that was for a ten-year-old boy—with the preacher puffing out condemnations in a rhythmic chant—the images of hundreds of souls saved and baptized and even healed stuck with me all these years.

Mercy was in need of such a revival. *I* was in need of a revival. Years of Grayson's one-note obsession with the poor had left my spirit parched. I was as dry as the bones Ezekiel saw in the valley. If a prophetic word from God could bring those dry bones to life, it didn't seem unreasonable that he could restore mine as well.

As soon as I walked into the tent, I felt like I was home. People were milling about and an older gentleman in a dress shirt and tie said "God bless you" as he handed me a paper fan and an envelope for the offering. "Victory in Jesus" was coming through the speakers and I looked at the stage to find Sandy Bell at the keyboard. I wondered how many other people from New Hope I would see at the revival, those who had left New Hope years ago and moved on to other churches. It was unlikely that many from Ignite would come—old-fashioned revivals weren't their style. Of course, it was virtually guaranteed that Grayson wouldn't be there.

As I made my way down the aisle to find a seat, I saw Miss Addie sitting with people from her group home. She had gotten so frail and her sweet voice had become raspy, but she still carried a joy in her smile. I stopped to say hello and give her a gentle hug. "It's been a long time since we've been to one of these, hasn't it?" I shouted to her over the music. She patted my hand and smiled.

"Makes me miss your mama," she said. I nodded. The image of my typically reserved mother with her hands lifted in praise made me smile as well. Already I could feel tendons connecting dry bone to dry bone, could feel withered spiritual muscle begin to grow and strengthen. I gave Miss Addie another gentle hug and told her that if I didn't see her again after the service I'd stop by and see her soon.

The crowd was beginning to get ready for the service, so I found a seat next to a young couple and their two small children. The little girl, who was maybe four and sitting in her mother's lap, looked up at me with a sticky grin from her half-eaten sucker. I made a funny face at her and she giggled before burying her tiny face in her mother's neck.

Several people took the stage and when a young man walked up to the podium, the crowd quieted down. "Well, I didn't know I had that much power," he said to a smattering of laughter. "Now let's all stand and sing some hymns." Sandy, who was still at the keyboard, starting playing "When the Roll is Called up Yonder" and then "There's Power in the Blood." With every note I sang, I felt life being breathed into my soul. Before I even realized what was happening, my hands were raised high in the air in complete surrender to the Spirit.

After the crowd sang a couple of hymns, we sat while one of the local choirs filed onto the risers at the back of the stage. And then a gray-headed man with a familiar flat top stood in front of the choir. As I watched his arm move in fluid motion, I had to force back a burning anger that tried to invade my peace. Tom Slater, like so many others, had been driven away by Grayson—had been discarded as old-fashioned and useless. Even people like Tom, who had been loyal defenders, eventually found themselves victims of Grayson's ego.

I had stayed at Ignite longer than I should have. Foolishly I believed that Grayson would either grow tired of Mercy or Mercy would grow tired of him. I was wrong on both counts. Even though I had waited patiently, had bided my time waiting for him to end up on a hook, he somehow always managed to wriggle away. No matter how many good people left the church, if five or ten more took their place, the leadership team didn't seem to care.

Leaving had never been an option I seriously considered. That church was in my blood. It was a birthright, but Grayson cheated me out of it just as surely as Jacob had swindled Esau out of his. He stole my blessing, too, and he tried to silence my voice—to keep me from exposing the truth about his self-centered ways. For a long time, I managed to get my licks in, mainly because he could never seem to replace me as the chair of the deacons, though he certainly tried. Finally he convinced enough people at the church to replace the deacons with a leadership team, at least as far as managing church business.

"This is a model for many churches these days," he said at a town hall meeting at the church. "Biblically, deacons were intended to be servants, to take care of the widows and orphans, as it were. It makes more sense to free them of the mundane decision making of the church and restore them to this necessary and important biblical role."

A couple of people stood to praise the idea, while others around them nodded their heads in sheep-like approval. Most of them hadn't grown up in church and didn't really understand the ways churches functioned—and they certainly couldn't conceive of Grayson's ultimate motive. But I knew the truth.

"You may have convinced them of your reasons," I said when I stood up. "You may have even convinced yourself. But the truth is, the deacons have always been a thorn in your side because we rein you in—or at least we try."

"It's not personal, Reed," Grayson said, trying to mask the irritation in his voice.

"It's always been personal. You hate it when people like me tell you you're wrong." Grayson shifted from foot to foot as I spoke. "And you're wrong a lot, by the way."

"That's unfair," a voice behind me said. It was Charlie Eversole.

"I guess he's already tapped you for his new leadership team," I shot back.

"As a matter of fact, no, he hasn't. If you'd stop trying to stir things up all the time, maybe you'd see all the good that is happening around here. Maybe you'd be a happier person."

"Quit making an ass of yourself," I said, forgetting to censor myself in the Lord's house—even if it was called a *worship center* now.

"Guys, please—" Grayson tried to interject, his face flushed red.

"You all are welcome to keep following this fool, but I'm done." I grabbed my jacket and stormed out, knocking my chair over in the process. Even though it had been nearly a year since it happened, that moment played out in my mind over and over with the intensity of a desert sun. It had evaporated my peace, leaving anger and bitterness to take root instead. As those emotions flourished, my spirit withered. I had let them live there too long.

The tent had grown quiet as the choir filed off the stage. Only a few coughs and the sounds of babies crying were heard as the preacher for the night—a short, stocky red-headed man from Tennessee—moved to the podium. He placed his Bible on the podium, and then grabbed the sides of it with his hands and leaned forward.

"Friends, I'm here to tell you that if you are a child of God, you're going to experience suffering. If you're following Jesus, you're going to experience persecution for his sake. But don't despair. And if you haven't yet accepted the loving yoke of the Father, I'm here to tell you that you don't have to be afraid to do it. Yes, you may suffer persecution, too. But here is the good news, my friend. Jesus says, 'Blessed are they which are persecuted for righteousness' sake: for theirs is the kingdom of heaven. Blessed are ye, when men shall revile you, and persecute you, and shall say all manner of evil against you falsely, for my sake. Rejoice, and be exceeding glad: for great is your reward in heaven: for so persecuted they the prophets which were before you.' Yes, my friends, though you may be persecuted for his sake then, glory hallelujah, you will also be blessed."

Shouts of “amen” and “praise Jesus” were lifted up from all over the tent and continued as the preacher moved into his rhythmic condemnations of the evils that come against God’s people. The presence of God filled the air and I felt it, but I also felt the presence of my dear mother, whose soft “hallelujah” whispered in my ear and cradled my soul. “Be at peace,” she whispered. And I was—for the first time in a long time—at peace. Even after the service, when I saw Fred Taylor—who seemed to ignore me even though I’d been told he’d finally seen Grayson for what he was—even then I smiled warmly at him with a newfound blessedness. Grayson was no longer going to steal my peace.

FRED

EFFIE AND I LEFT the church for exactly three weeks. We slipped away quietly, though we suspected that our absence would raise questions. It did, for a few folks. Effie got stopped twice in stores and once at the library. A few people called to make sure we were all right. "We heard Effie was fired," they'd say. Or "Did Grayson really tell Effie to quit or he'd have to fire her?" A couple of people even brought up the rumors of an affair. We were quick to set the record straight. Not that it stops anyone from talking.

I was a ship without a rudder after we left Ignite. The current pushed me toward an empty horizon with only a vague promise of what might be beyond it. But my heart longed to return to shore, to the security of the known—only I didn't know how to get there. When a county-wide tent revival was held at the fairgrounds a couple of weeks after we left Ignite, I thought it might help me find direction.

The tent was nearly full when Effie and I arrived. Some ushers were just setting out chairs in the back. "Great crowd," one of them smiled as he motioned for us to sit. He handed us a fan with a quick "God bless you" before hurrying off to seat others as they came in. I looked around and saw a few people I knew. In a small town, it's hard to go anywhere without knowing at least a few folks. When the service started, and a young man got up to lead the music, I saw that Sandy Bell was playing the keyboard. I hadn't seen her for a few years but she looked nearly the same. She certainly seemed happy behind that keyboard. Most people I knew who had left Ignite were happy and doing well. So why did I feel so unsettled?

The hymns were familiar, like home, and the rhythm of the preacher transported me back to my grandmother's church, when I would get swept up, not in the frantic, impassioned delivery of the preacher, but in the rhythmic and gentle chorus of "hallelujah" and "praise Jesus" Grandma would utter in response. At one time, I would have found comfort in that memory, as sweet as it was and as much as I adored my grandmother, but now it was like looking into a broken mirror in which I was barely recognizable.

The revival preacher spoke of persecution but it was forgiveness that saturated my thoughts. "Forgiveness is a powerful gift if we are the person who has done wrong, but when we are the person who has been wronged, forgiveness is the most humbling and challenging acts of spiritual obedience." When Grayson spoke those words the last time I was at Ignite, I knew that although he meant them for his congregation they were also deeply personal to him. He had been wronged so many times since he had come to Mercy. How often had he needed to offer that gift to others?

Yet even as the fevered pitch of the revival preacher reached its crescendo, it was Grayson's words that brought me to my knees. Without even being aware of it, I had been angry at Grayson. Angry that he wasn't more concerned how his actions impacted others. Angry that he let Effie feel guilty over such a minor infraction. Angry that he had not come to us, as close as we had been, to make it right. Not even knowing it, I had been waiting for him. But forgiveness is willful not passive, Grayson had preached. *Willful not passive.*

As music filled the tent, as the preacher called for every head to be bowed and every eye closed, as he urged people to act in response to the Spirit, my heart pumped those words through my body until the weight of them dropped me to my knees, right there at my seat. I felt Effie's hand on my shoulder.

When the song was over and the preacher gave praise for the souls that had come forward to profess salvation or to rededicate themselves to the Lord, I stood and wiped away the tears that had come from my surrender to the spiritual act of forgiveness.

"Are you all right?" Effie whispered and grasped my hand.

"I am now," I said, giving her hand a squeeze. "Let's go home." She nodded, but it was only later that she realized I didn't mean our little brick house on Center Street.

BLESSED ARE THOSE WHO ARE PERSECUTED

REED

THE PARK HAD ALWAYS been a treasure for the community. The land had been donated to the city by one of the founding families. Over the years, the city added a couple of picnic shelters, a playground, and most recently a jogging path. The Women's Club takes great care to plant and tend some of the prettiest flower beds in this part of the country. It was the perfect place for families and schools and churches to gather because it was clean and safe. But that was before the homeless people took it over.

Years ago, the vagrants stayed out by the railroad tracks or down in the old warehouses and abandoned factories. They respected their boundaries. They were rarely seen near schools or churches, and certainly not the park. But then they started coming into the good areas of town, wandering the streets and hanging out in doorways—often with their hand out trying to scam good, hardworking people out of money. They started sleeping on park benches before getting bolder by setting up tents, like the park was some kind of campground. Even after the city passed an ordinance and cleared out the tents, they'd be right back up a few days later. Of course parents stopped taking their children to the park and forget women walking or jogging there.

Grayson Armstrong was at the heart of the problem. From the moment he set foot in Mercy, he showed he valued those people more than he did other people in our community—even people in his own congregation. He encouraged those people to receive handouts instead of getting a job. Learned helplessness is what they call that. If I hadn't stopped it, he would have gladly turned the church into a homeless shelter with no thought to the safety of the people he was supposed to be taking care of. So I wasn't surprised that he was right in the middle of what was going on at the park.

My house backs up to the park, so more than most people in town, I knew everything that was going on there. The first time the tents popped up, I called the police, but they said there wasn't anything they could do. It wasn't against the law. So I called the mayor. Marvin grew up down the street from me, so I figured he'd help me get something done. That's how we got the ordinance passed. After that, when I called the police, they not only came but stood over those vagrants while they took down the tents and hauled them out of there. I watched it all from my back deck.

But then before long I'd start seeing tents again. One time I looked over there and saw a familiar face. I hadn't seen Grayson in months, but there he was bringing bags of food out of his car and handing them to the people who gathered around. He was laughing and patting people on the back. I tried to imagine him being that friendly with the church folk, but I couldn't. A feeling that I thought I'd buried began to seep to the surface, and the more I watched him the more I hated him, especially when I saw him glance my way and smile. That's when I decided to talk to Marvin again.

"You know, it doesn't help to take those tent cities down if we have well-meaning people taking food to them," I said. Grayson wasn't well-meaning but it didn't help my cause to say otherwise. "It doesn't give those vagrants any incentive to leave and stay away. It's like feeding a stray dog."

"I see your point, Reed. I'll see what I can do."

When the City Council met to vote on a new ordinance banning food sharing, the small council room was full. People were even squeezed against the back wall and they were holding signs and wearing lime green shirts. I heard they were threatening a protest if the ordinance passed. Some of the people were from Ignite. I looked around and sure enough there was Grayson sitting on the front row in his green shirt. Not that I was surprised. I was surprised, though, to see Fred and Effie sitting next to him. I guessed they had kissed and made up. *Well good for them,* I sneered to myself. Even more surprising was seeing my own pastor sitting up there with them. I thought he had better judgment than that. *Well no matter,* I thought. *I don't care if I'm the only one speaking in favor of the ordinance.*

The meeting started well enough, but when it was time to discuss the ordinance, when the people in support of it stood to speak, the crowd became rowdy. They even shouted down Mrs. Campbell, my eighty-year-old neighbor. I looked at Marvin and he finally said he'd clear the room if the outbursts continued. After Mrs. Campbell spoke, I stood and walked to the podium. I glanced at Grayson, just to let him know that he wasn't going to get the better of me, and then I turned my attention to the Council.

"I am here tonight to tell you a story—my story. I've lived in Mercy all my life, not just because I was born here, but because it's a great community. Or at least it was. We have let certain groups, certain people, change who we are. We let them coddle junkies and alcoholics and make them believe it's okay to turn nice neighborhoods into shanty towns. It's no longer safe." Several of the Council members nodded. "That's why this Council wisely passed an ordinance to prohibit these vagrants from setting up camps in places like the park. And it's helped. But these tent cities will keep popping up as long as people—well-meaning people—take food and supplies to them. I ask you to consider the welfare of good citizens like Mrs. Campbell and put a stop to this practice."

A few people clapped when I finished. Mrs. Campbell gave me a sweet smile when I sat down. That's when I knew that no matter what happened that night I had done the right thing. Sometimes, to be perfectly honest, I got so bogged down in my feelings toward Grayson that I forgot that it wasn't just a battle between the two of us. I was fighting for the Addie's and Mrs. Campbell's of Mercy. Maybe that's why I wasn't bothered when it was Grayson's turn to speak, even when he made it personal.

"Just because Mr. Hyden says there's a problem doesn't make it so," he said. Though his back was to me, I could imagine his sanctimonious grin. "I'm guessing he hasn't even been close enough to 'those people' to know anything about them," he continued. But he sounded like a fool. I had practically lived with these people in my backyard for months. I had seen the trash they left behind, like the whisky bottles that had been thrown into my yard. I had smelled the stench of their unwashed bodies and the way they had made the park an open sewer.

The Council recognized Grayson's foolishness for what it was and passed the ordinance. Mrs. Campbell gave me a hug before she left. "Thank you," she whispered. I carried that hug with me as I walked past Grayson.

As soon as the ordinance went into effect, the tents were gone and so were the people—all of them. I was finally able to enjoy a peaceful summer afternoon with no worries. I could sit on my deck and not feel afraid or disgusted. But as usual Grayson showed his disregard for anything he didn't agree with. At first, I just thought he was setting up for a church picnic or maybe a family reunion. He and some others set up a long row of tables just outside one of the shelters, which struck me as odd. But it was Grayson, so odd was almost normal for him. Not long after they had filled the tables with food, people started trickling in. They seemed like regular folk at first, but then I noticed the scruffy beards and disheveled clothing. *Only Grayson would show such blatant contempt for me, not to mention the law,* I thought. Not that I was about to let him get away with it. I marched right down to fence row and called him over.

"It's a beautiful day for a picnic," he said when he got closer.

"Entertaining new church members?" I said, hoping he recognized the sarcasm in my voice.

"As a matter of fact, I am. You're welcome to join us." He smiled. I did not.

"You're breaking the law," I said.

"It's an unjust law and you know it."

"But it *is* the law. Just because Grayson Armstrong doesn't like it doesn't change that." I would have waited for a response, but I had never known Grayson to admit he was wrong. "I'm calling the police," I said as I turned back toward my house.

"Do what you need to do," he said. "I'll keep doing what I need to do."

When the police arrived, they talked to people in the crowd. I could see Grayson's relaxed stance as he chatted with an officer. Even when the officer handed him a citation, he shook the officer's hand, stuffed the citation in his pocket, and went back to the food table like the police weren't even there.

It wasn't the last time Grayson found himself in trouble with the law.

MARVIN

Reed had told me all I needed to know about Grayson Armstrong. Not that he really needed to. I had seen Mr. Armstrong in action enough over the past few years since he was a frequent visitor to City Council meetings. We could count on him to show up anytime we discussed the county health clinic services or race relations or, especially, vagrancy. Sometimes I wondered how he ever had time for his congregation, but after listening to Reed, I knew the answer was that he didn't.

I wasn't surprised when he came to the meeting about the food sharing ordinance. He had called my office several times in the days leading up to the meeting. That night, he gave a long-winded speech, as usual. I swear that man loves to hear himself talk. I guess preachers can't help themselves, although some people would laugh at a politician saying such a thing.

As usual—no, it was really worse than usual—he didn't talk *to* us, he talked *at* us. More like lectured us, all high and mighty. He also managed to get some jabs at Reed in the process. "That's his true character," Reed said later. "He thinks he's fooling people, but thank goodness not everyone is that gullible." Most of the Council wasn't. The vote wasn't even that close.

I should have known, though, that wouldn't be the end of it.

EFFIE

Everyone was linked arm in arm in front of the courthouse steps, stretching from one corner of the building to the other. Up and down the line was a wall of bright green shirts emblazoned with a red circle encompassing a backslash over top of the words "For I was hungry." Across the street, a group of city workers, including the mayor, gathered, trying to figure out what to do. The mayor stood off to one side talking on his phone, his arms flailing while he spoke. His words weren't clear but his voice still carried over to us. He was up to something. All we could do was stand firm and wait.

It didn't take long.

Three police cars pulled up in front of the courthouse with their lights flashing. My stomach tightened. The officers emerged from their cars and all but one of them came and stood in a line in front of us, about twenty feet away. They stood with their feet slightly apart, their hands cupped together in front of their bodies, and their eyes staring straight ahead. Their guns were still in the holsters but visible. I could feel my heart thumping faster. The other officer had gone across the street to the mayor. They talked and we waited. Somewhere down the line of linked arms, someone softly chanted "Shame on you." And then a few more voices joined the chant until the whole line was shouting.

"Shame on you! Shame on you! Shame on you!"

The officer who had been talking with the mayor came across the street and headed straight for Grayson, who was standing next to me. I recognized the officer. He and his family had been to Ignite a few times. He was also one of the officers that had given us citations when we were handing out food in the park.

"Good morning, Officer Stone," Grayson said. His arms were still linked with mine and Jamal Brown's.

"Good morning, Rev. Armstrong," he said. He was all business but there was still warmth in his eyes. "I'm hoping we can avoid a confrontation today, so I need you and your group to allow an unobstructed path into the building." The officer relaxed a bit. "I know that you're an honorable man and you're a law-abiding citizen. It will make everything easier if you simply comply with this order. I'm hoping that you will want to be an example to these people."

"They are the ones who are an example to me," Grayson said. "The ordinance against feeding the homeless is unjust. These people know it, and they're willing to stand against it. I'm proud to stand alongside them, no matter what happens here today."

"If you don't comply, we'll be forced to take action. Neither of us wants that to happen."

"Do what you must, Officer Stone. I don't hold it against you."

They looked at each other. There was nothing more to be done except what had to be done. Neither side was backing down. Officer Stone motioned and the other officers joined him.

"I'm asking you one more time to open a pathway to the courthouse," Officer Stone said. His eyes pleaded with us. When we didn't respond, an officer reached for Grayson's arm and tried to jerk him free. It wasn't difficult because Grayson didn't resist. His arm slipped from mine and he stepped forward with his arms behind his back, preparing for the inevitable. Jamal tried to grab Grayson's arm to keep him in line, but he lunged forward instead and fell into an officer who had his back turned to us. The officer whirled around and he and Jamal tumbled to the ground. The man who had been next to Jamal shoved another officer who had come to help. Instinctively, I jumped back out of the way.

"Stop!" Grayson shouted as he rushed to control the man. "Not this way, Ryan," he said. "We're not going to do it this way." The man still tried to lunge forward, but Grayson blocked him. He finally calmed down and took a step backward. By this time, there was a sea of green shirts surrounding us. People were pushing and pulling one another until it was like the ebb and flow of the tide. The noise of the commotion mingled with an occasional shout from a protestor or a command from an officer. I was shuffled to the back of the crowd until I lost sight of Grayson. I tried to squeeze my way back through the crowd but had no luck so I worked my way toward the end of the mass of green shirts. I hadn't gotten far when the crowd seemed to part like the Red Sea, leaving direct sight of Grayson standing in front of Officer Stone and the mayor. I moved as close as I dared. That's when I noticed Ryan and Jamal were in those plastic handcuffs with two officers by their sides.

"I want this one arrested, too," the mayor said, pointing to Grayson.

"For what? He hasn't interfered with us. In fact he tried to calm things down," Officer Stone responded.

"I don't care. He's the instigator for this group. He's responsible for their actions today and for their blatant defiance of a duly adopted city ordinance ever since it was passed."

"But..."

"Officer, I expect you to do your sworn duty."

"It's all right," Grayson said, holding out his wrists.

Officer Stone slipped the cuffs over Grayson's wrists. "I'm sorry," he said.

"Grayson," I called out, ready to take a step forward. He shook his head and I stopped.

"It'll be okay," he said. He smiled to reassure me it would be.

As I watched him being put in the police car, I stood frozen in place. Even as the other protesters began to slip away, I couldn't move. I wasn't sure what to do, so I just watched until the police car was out of sight. Had we done the right thing, I wondered, especially the way the events had unfolded. But Grayson's words to the City Council echoed in my head.

"If Mr. Hyden has ever been in close enough proximity to those homeless people to know anything about them, he would know that they are the most vulnerable among us. They are veterans who have served our country. They are women—and even children—who have escaped abusive homes. They are people who suffer from depression and anxiety. And, yes, some are addicted to drugs or alcohol. But the common thread is that 'they' are people—human beings with human needs. All we are asking is that we continue to be allowed to treat them with dignity."

That dignity was worth fighting for. If nothing else, Grayson had shown me that.

NATALIE

After the chaotic rush to get Blake and Hannah off to school every morning, I headed to the basement to paint. The beauty of seeing an emotion come to life on a canvas makes me know that I'm alive. And creating something that is a part of me but also apart from me makes me appreciate God's creative dimension. *In the beginning God created.* He hovered over the waters in darkness ready to call forth the light.

I opened the yellow and orange paints, ready to bring autumn to life on the blank canvas. It's always magical to watch seemingly random dots of yellow and orange transform into trees, to feel in control of the process but also to experience the total surrender to the creation taking its own form. I stepped back from the painting, pleased with the morning's work. I had just put the paints and brushes away when the phone rang.

"He's been arrested," Effie breathlessly said when I answered.

"Effie? Slow down, I can't understand you. Did you say arrested?"

"Yes, Grayson's been arrested along with two other men at the protest. It was the mayor who insisted on it. They took him away in a police car. Oh, Natalie, what are we going to do?"

"It's okay, Effie. I'll head over to the police station." I hung up and slipped out of my paint shirt and headed upstairs. Tyler, who was home for summer break, was just coming downstairs.

"I'm heading to the police station to get your dad," I said.

"The police station? Is he okay?"

"I'm not sure. Something happened at the protest this morning."

"Of course it did," he said. Maybe I should have responded to that, but there was hurt that lay at the bottom of that sarcasm—a hurt that put my mother's heart in conflict with my wife's heart.

"Do you want me to go with you?" he asked, seeing the worry in my eyes.

"I'll be all right, but thanks for asking. Besides, you have to be at work soon."

"I can call in."

I shook my head and wrapped my arms around him. "I'm glad you're home," I whispered.

The sky was blue on my drive to the police station. Not azure blue like a robin's egg, but grayish blue like a sheet of waxed paper stretched from one horizon to the other. It was a blue that would have foretold rain even if droplets weren't gathering on the windshield. It was a blue that anticipated my mood.

For days, I carried a sense of dread with me. Between the fights at City Hall, the citations while feeding the homeless, and now Grayson's arrest at the protest, I was drained. Ministry sucks the marrow right out of your bones. It leaves you depleted with no resources to replenish yourself. Too often anymore it felt that way. After fifteen years in ministry, most of them in Mercy, I was weary. Nothing had been easy in Mercy. If it had been up to me, we would have left a long time ago—and it wouldn't have been just leaving Mercy. We would have left the church behind, too. Grayson would have a nice nine-to-five job and we would live in a quiet, secluded place in the country. Away from people and away from problems. Sometimes I said that out loud to Grayson. He'd smile and say, "That sounds nice. When do we leave?" "I'm ready right now," I'd say. We'd laugh, because we knew we weren't going anywhere.

This is what we had been called to do, but as I drove toward the police station I looked to the darkening heavens anyway and begged God to release us from it. As if in response, the heavens opened up and sent big, fat raindrops crashing to earth.

I pulled into the police station and shut off the motor. The rain pounded against the car with such force that it sounded like static on an old television with the volume all the way up. For a time, the heavy rain obscured nearly everything, like a curtain had been drawn around me. It was strangely comforting being shrouded from the world, if only for a moment.

When the rain slowed considerably, I fished in the floorboard for an umbrella and made a dash into the station. The woman at the front desk told me they were processing Grayson, which could take a while. I wasn't sure what to expect, but I was afraid to ask her. So I took a seat, picked up a magazine, and began thumbing through it. Every time the door behind the woman opened I thought it might be Grayson in handcuffs being led off to jail, but it was just an officer heading out to the patrol cars. Finally, Grayson emerged. He was alone. He smiled when he saw me.

"I'm glad to see you," he said.

"I bet you are." I didn't know whether to be angry or relieved. "Are you free to go?"

"Yes," he said as he looked back at the woman at the desk to confirm. She nodded.

The sun, which had returned while I was waiting, blinded us as we left the building, and I shielded my eyes. I followed Grayson, who climbed into the passenger seat of the car while I got behind the wheel. We sat for a few seconds, letting the strangeness of the moment hang between us, before he finally spoke.

"Well, I hope your day is going better than mine," he said. He looked at me with that boyish smile, and I couldn't help but laugh.

"It was going well until I had to come bail someone out. Did they throw the book at you?"

"They just gave us a citation. I'm sure the mayor won't be happy about that."

"You're lucky, you know."

"I know," he said as he grabbed my hand.

I dropped him off at his car, which he'd left near the courthouse. He said he had something quick to do at the office, and then he'd be home. The house was quiet when I returned. Tyler had left for work and Blake and Hannah wouldn't be home from school for a few more hours. Even though the laundry was waiting for me, I was drawn again to the basement. I stood in front of the autumn scene I had painted that morning. The bright colors were vivid and full of expectancy. But what they waited for was the dark underside of autumn—the preparation for death. I shivered and grabbed my paint shirt, pulling it tight around me. I picked up a brush and the figure of a woman began to emerge under the trees. Her arm was outstretched, ready to take hold of a figure not yet on the canvas.

"You're so beautiful when you paint," Grayson said as he stood in the doorway.

"You startled me." My face flushed red. It didn't matter how long we had been together, it still made me feel self-conscious to hear him say such things. Especially when I had pulled my hair back without even running a comb though it and hadn't put make up on before I left the house that morning. I was a mess in that old paint shirt. But he didn't seem to mind. He came up behind me and slipped his arms around my waist. I felt his breath on my neck as he kissed it, and I melted back into him. I turned to him, the paint brush still in my hand, and kissed him full on the mouth. He drew back for a moment, his eyes searching mine, and then he pressed his lips hard against mine, like he was terrified I was going to disappear. His hands fumbled for the buttons on my paint shirt. I giggled and stepped back.

"Let me do that," I said. "I'd also better get rid of this." I laid the paint brush on the table and then unbuttoned the shirt. We both slipped out of our clothes and came together again, our bodies submitting to their hunger for one another as we dropped to the floor. When we were finished, we lay entwined. I could feel his heart racing. It was my heart. Mine was his.

"You're shivering," he said. "Let me get something to put over us."

"No," I said. "Just hold me."

He pulled me to him tighter. Over his shoulder, I saw the woman with her outstretched hand, waiting. Even in Grayson's arms, I trembled at the harbinger of winter coming.

TONYA

Grayson Armstrong seemed to always be tilting at windmills. Personally, I don't think he was happy unless he drummed up some enemy to fight or some cause to defend. Sitting on the City Council, I saw him on a regular basis. He certainly had his defenders on the Council, but I wasn't one of them. He was a nice guy, don't get me wrong. But how many times did we have to be told that we weren't doing anything right in Mercy? Nothing like an outsider coming in and telling all the yokels how to do things. We'd all have been better off if he had just stuck to preaching to his congregation.

RAMIE

I ARRIVED IN TENNESSEE just before Mommy passed. Jim knew I was coming but still seemed surprised when he opened the front door. I guess it was because I was a little girl the last time he'd seen me. After a moment, though, he threw open his arms and gave me a big hug, but I didn't hug him back. I didn't want his hug. I had come for Naomi's sake, not his.

"I'm so glad you're here, sweetie," he said with his plastic, preacher smile. "Come in. Come in." He put his arm around my shoulder and ushered me inside. I stepped into the living room, which was dreary despite the white walls. The heavy furniture was formal—Early American or maybe Victorian. It didn't matter. Either way, I couldn't imagine that much living went on in that room. I looked back at Jim. His face had grown solemn. "Your mother's not doing well," he said. "I can take you to her." He grabbed my hand and started to lead me toward the kitchen. He expected me to follow, but I stood still, like my feet were nailed to the floor. Jim looked puzzled, like he couldn't understand why I had come all that way just to stand in the doorway.

"She's had a long drive, Dad. Maybe she just needs to sit for a minute." A red-headed girl appeared in the kitchen doorway. "Hi. I'm Naomi," she said. She smiled, and my knees buckled at the echo of my mother staring back at me. "I can take care of Ramie if you want to go back and sit with Mom. I'll bring her back when she's ready." Jim nodded obediently and disappeared through the kitchen. Naomi smiled at me again, and I was struck by how old she seemed—like she was the big sister taking care of me. The presence of death will do that to you, make you grow up fast.

"Do you want something to drink?" she said as she motioned for me to sit on one of the stiff chairs.

I shook my head and sat down. I was as stiff as the chair.

She shrugged her shoulders and plopped down on the couch and, with that, she was fifteen again. She was prettier in person than in her picture. Her hair was in a long braid off to one side and her face was fresh and natural. She was wearing jeans and a T-shirt with what appeared to be her high school mascot on the front. We sat in awkward silence. We were strangers.

"Did you have any trouble finding the place," she finally said.

"No, your directions were very good." I smiled at her. Maybe Grayson was right, I thought. Maybe Naomi was the key to my peace. As comforting as that should have been, I couldn't shake the selfishness of that thought. My peace would likely come at the expense of Naomi's. I knew that I couldn't give her what she needed, much less what she wanted. But it was too late to think about that.

"How's your mother…our mother?" I said.

"Not good." Her eyes widened as she blinked back tears.

"It's okay, honey." It was strange to be offering comfort to her. Not because I didn't want to comfort her, but because my words had reached a mirror and were reflected back to me. I was that girl—curled up on the couch into a cocoon-like lump—feeling ancient but desperately trying to recapture a future that had been stolen from me.

"They say it could be any time now," Naomi said. "She's not been conscious, which I suppose is a blessing. Dad thinks so anyway. We told her it was okay to let go." Her voice carried the weight of the tears falling down her cheeks, which she wiped away with the back of her fist. "But she's been hanging on for days. I told her you were coming. I think she's been waiting for you."

I shifted in my chair. I didn't want her to be waiting for me. If she was waiting because she hoped to get absolution from me, she wasn't going to find it. If she was waiting to get a good-bye from me, she shouldn't have bothered. She had thrown away a chance for a good-bye when she walked out more than twenty years before without ever offering one. Whatever she may have been waiting for, I wasn't the one who could give it to her. *It was a mistake for me to come,* I thought. But then Naomi's expectant eyes were searching mine, trying urgently to find hope. I knew that look. I had seen it on my father's face too many times.

"Do you want to see her now?" she asked.

My heart screamed in protest, but I nodded in defiance of my heart. *I have faith in you*, Grayson had said. It had to have been that faith that drove one foot in front of the other, to follow the tall red headed girl—my sister—through the kitchen and into the den in the back of the house. Nothing else could have compelled me into that dimly lit room.

The curtains on the two windows were drawn tight and the only light in the room was from a floor lamp beside a hospital type bed. The room already smelled of decaying flesh. The only sound was the rhythmic breathing, that sounded like the whooshing of a machine, coming from the bed. Jim was sitting in a chair, reading what looked like a Bible. He looked up and when he saw me, he stood and moved to the foot of the bed. I would have been fine staying right there at the edge of the room, but Naomi took my hand and led me to the side of the bed.

"Look who's here, Mom," she said, her voice cracked but she tried to sound cheerful. "It's Ramie. Ramie's come to see you, just like in your dream."

I felt sick to my stomach. I wanted to run from there and right out the front door without even looking back, but Naomi squeezed my hand. I moved closer to the rail and looked down at the frail woman lying there. Her face was swollen and all of her beautiful hair was gone. There was nothing familiar about her. Nothing. Nothing to hate. Nothing to love. There was only a stranger.

"I think she knows you're here," Naomi whispered. I didn't see how. There had been no response from Mommy. "The nurse told us that she probably can hear us. She told us to keep talking to her." Naomi nodded at me.

I cleared my throat. "It's Ramie. I'm here." As soon as the words slipped from my mouth, Mommy let out one long breath and then there was nothing. No sound. No movement in her chest. I looked at Naomi and saw the panic in her eyes. Jim rushed to the other side of the bed. "Nan," he called to her, and as if in response, she sucked in another breath before expelling one final long breath. We stood for a moment, watching. Waiting. Another breath never came. I stared at her, this thing that I had hated. This wayfaring stranger. This phantom who had haunted my thoughts. I wanted to feel something—anything. Hate, fear, pity, even love. But there was just emptiness. Not even Naomi's weeping plucked any emotion from the depths of my emptiness. I turned my eyes away and was suddenly aware of the strangeness of the place. I didn't belong there.

So I left.

I left so fast that I nearly knocked over the boys—her sons—as they were coming into the room. I didn't stop to greet them or even say anything to Naomi. There wasn't anything to say anyway. The only *bond* between us had been broken, and it wasn't even a real bond, only a bloodline.

I was restless for days after I got home. Something felt unfinished. A weariness sank into my bones, and I felt like I was drowning. Every time I tried to come up for air, I was pulled back into the murky waters. I would have given up—was ready to give up—and let the despair swallow me up, but Grayson wouldn't let me. Not that he knew he was doing anything. I hadn't even told him that I'd gone to see Naomi or that Mommy had died. How could I when I was still wrestling with everything about that visit? But every time I was ready to give into the despair, he'd come into the diner and flash that big smile that made everything seem better. It was like somehow he could sense when I needed it most.

He had long since stopped inviting me to church. We had come to an understanding about me and those big red buildings with steeples on top. He laughed when I described it that way, but not in a mean way. "Church isn't a building. It's the people," he said.

"Well, I don't care much for the people in the building, either," I said. We both laughed.

So no one was more surprised than I was when I decided to go to Grayson's church. For days I had stared out the diner window at that red brick church across the street and watched him come and go—watched him stop and talk with people, even put his hand on their shoulder and bow his head in prayer. I envied the comfort that it seemed to bring.

When Sunday came, I was more nervous than I expected. Even choosing what to wear became intimidating. Grayson had once said that services were very casual, but when I had gone to church with Mommy, men wore ties and women were always in dresses. I knew Grayson's church was nothing like that one—at least not the way he described it—but I still couldn't imagine wearing anything but a dress. I wasn't prepared for seeing people in jeans and even shorts. I also wasn't prepared for a religious service in what looked like a music hall. The walls were black except for the backdrop on the stage, which was made of thin strips of light-colored wood in a brick-like pattern. Blue and yellow lights focused on the keyboard, microphone stands, and drums. Rows of padded chairs, in three sections, faced the stage. It was definitely not like the church I'd gone to with Mommy. I didn't even see a place where people could be baptized.

People were milling about and chatting with one another. I found a seat on the end of the back row, in case I needed to get out of there quick. A few people stopped to tell me they were glad to see me, but I would have been just fine if they had left me alone. I was glad when the service started and they turned down the lights. It was good to be obscured by the darkness, to observe without being observed.

When the band started playing, and everyone stood and clapped to the rhythm, I thought of Daddy. Even though he wasn't a church-going man, he would have liked this music. He might have even been up there on stage. With that comforting thought drifting in my mind, I surrendered to the music. The drumbeat sank into my chest and compelled my heart to beat faster and faster. I was being thrust upward, ready to break through the water's surface, ready to fill my lungs with a new breath. Even when a man slipped by me during one of the songs, breaking the feeling for a moment, and even after the music stopped, my heart tried to linger in the weightlessness of it all.

Grayson took the stage. In all the time I had known him, had known he was a preacher, strangely I had never pictured him actually preaching. Maybe because he wasn't like any preacher I had ever known. He had always just been Grayson. But he seemed to fit up there on that stage just as well as he had in the diner, and I was as captivated by him as ever, by the calming sound of his voice. Even when he began speaking about forgiveness, or when the image of my mother's lifeless body filled my mind, or when the rush of anger washed over me because of it, I focused on the sound of Grayson's voice.

"Forgiveness is a powerful gift if we are the person who has done wrong. But when we are the person who has been wronged, forgiveness is the most humbling and challenging act of spiritual obedience. The reason is because forgiveness means that you give up all claim to that which you are owed. That means you may have to live without restitution or even a simple apology. But the reason it's important to forgive anyway is because when you hold on to that claim, when you are determined to get what you are owed no matter what, you not only close off a pathway to reconciliation, you close off a pathway to your own healing. You carry it around—that hurt and anger—because you're afraid if you leave it behind it's the same as saying it was okay for them to hurt you. Of course it's not okay, but you are the one who is weighted down by its burden. You are the one who can barely breathe under the weight of it."

It was as if he was reading my thoughts. Like he could feel the panic in my body as it longed for air. Tears fell down and burned my cheeks. My hands trembled. I had hated Mommy so long that I could barely remember what it was like not to feel the weight of it.

There is freedom from that burden, he said. You just have to trust the Father enough to let go of it.

I thought of my own daddy. When I was six, he taught me how to float on my back. I was so scared that I held his hand hard—squeezed it until my fingers turned white.

"You're okay, Ramie. I'm right here. Let go. You're okay."

"I can't, Daddy. What if I go under?"

"You'll be okay. Trust me. Just let go."

I loosened my grip and let my fingers drag across his hand until they reached the tips of his fingers. And then the feel of his warm flesh was gone, and I was on my own. The water moved quietly around me and for a time I was the water. Everything else dropped away, even Daddy. I was free.

As Grayson finished his message, his voice and Daddy's voice became one. "Let go, Ramie," they said. "It's time to let go."

TYLER

THE MUFFLED SOUNDS OF someone moving around in my room woke me up. I opened one eye to find Mom picking up piles of clothes from the floor and putting them in a laundry basket. I watched her for a few seconds as she tried to move in slow motion to avoid making sounds.

"I told you that you don't have to do that," I said as I finally rolled over.

"I'm sorry, honey. I didn't mean to wake you."

"You don't have to do my laundry, Mom."

"I know," she said as she threw another pair of jeans into the basket. "But now that you're in college, I don't have many opportunities to do things for you anymore, so just let me do it." She tapped my foot, sticking out from the covers, as she put the last shirt in the basket and headed for the door.

"Mom," I said, and she turned to look at me. "Thanks—for everything."

"You're very welcome, honey." She shut the door behind her and I let the drowsiness weave me in and out of sleep until Callie jumped onto the bed and put her paws on my chest. She meowed a few times and nudged my hand with her head. I stroked her fur and listened to her purr, and we were both content for a time. I knew it wouldn't last long, not with a six-year-old in the house. It didn't. Hannah came bursting through the door, sending Callie scurrying.

"Are you going to sleep all day?" Hannah said as she jumped up on the bed. "Come on. You said you would play with me and Daddy today."

"Yes, I did, didn't I." Her face lit up and she bounced some more. "Let me get dressed and I'll be right down." She bounded off the bed and out the door, leaving it wide open. I smiled, thinking how great it would be to have that much energy again.

I got up and closed the door, and then fumbled in the closet for a pair of jeans. It was comfortable to be home again after nine months away. It was also strange. I was a guest in my parents' home. Not that they treated me that way, and not that my room had changed at all while I was away. But the posters on the walls, the academic ribbons dangling from the knobs on the chest of drawers, the blue and green plaid bedspread, even the study desk with the small black chair felt like they belonged to someone else.

I was just putting on my T-shirt when I heard squeals out back. When I looked out the window, I saw Hannah running through the sprinkler. Every time she passed through the water, she squealed in delight. Dad was off to one side, dripping wet and cheering her on. *I'd better change into swim trunks,* I thought. When I got outside, I barely had enough time to slip off my shoes before Hannah grabbed my hand and drug me into the sprinkler.

"You have to jump like this," she said as she jumped over the sprinkler head and looked back at me to signal it was my turn. I followed her and pretended to be scared to jump. "You can do it, Tyler," she said. "Just close your eyes and jump." I squeezed my eyes shut and made an exaggerated jumping motion over the sprinkler. Hannah cheered and clapped. "Good job," she said. "Come on, Daddy. It's your turn," she hollered.

"Yeah, come on, Daddy," I called to him. "Don't be a chicken." Dad laughed and came barreling toward us and then in an exaggerated manner made a baby step over the sprinkler just as the water headed straight up. He caught a face full of water and fell backward in a fit of coughing and sputtering that transformed into a belly laugh.

"Well, that didn't work the way I thought it would," he said when he caught his breath.

Hannah squealed, "Do it again, Daddy," which made him start laughing all over again. I crumpled into a heap from laughing so hard. It had been a long time—maybe never—that I had laughed like that with Dad. Of course it was too much to think that our relationship had really changed, but I was determined to drink in that moment. Mom came out later to tell us it was time for lunch.

As she dried Hannah's hair with a towel, Hannah looked up at me, her bright blue eyes twinkling. "This is the best day ever," she declared. I smiled down at her. I try to remember that sweet face looking up at me. It was a face I had rarely recognized in myself—one of utter joy.

After lunch, Hannah went down for a nap, not that she wanted to. But I was glad for the time alone with Mom and Dad, especially since Blake wouldn't be home for a few more hours. Dad and Mom both picked up books. I sat for a while and watched them read, trying to decide if I really wanted to start the conversation I'd been building the courage to have. Finally, I cleared my throat.

"I've met someone at college," I said, hesitating a bit. Dad laid down his book and stared at me over the top of his reading glasses. "His name is Mark. He's a junior."

"That's great, honey," Mom said. But I never took my eyes off Dad. He looked like he'd just awakened from an unsettling dream.

"I'd like to invite him for Fourth of July, if that's okay," I said, refocusing on Mom.

"Of course. The more, the merrier. Right, dear," she said turning to Dad.

"Don't you think Blake might be uncomfortable? I mean, for boys his age, this kind of thing can be..." His voice trailed off.

"Blake's okay with it. I've already talked with him. You're the one who seems uncomfortable with it."

He pulled his reading glasses off and let them swing back and forth as he rolled the earpiece between his thumb and fingers. "I really don't know why you insist on always making these conversations into a confrontation," he said.

"Maybe I just want you to be honest with me about how you feel."

He scrunched up his face. "It's disappointing that you don't know how I feel. You guys are my world. It's just hard to—" His phone rang and he looked down. "I'd better take this. We'll talk about this later," he said as he stood and headed to the back deck. He seemed relieved to put off talking about it.

"Why does he have to be that way?" I asked Mom after he left.

"I think you're misinterpreting his reaction. He loves you and always will, no matter what. He's just under a lot of pressure. This is just a little inconvenient right now."

"So I'm an inconvenience?"

"That's not what I meant, honey. I'm sorry." She put her arm around my shoulder and gave me a slight squeeze. "I just hope you can understand that your dad has more to think about than you and me."

"You don't think I know that? I've watched him my whole life. You know what I've seen him do? I've seen him stand up to people who tried to bully him and shame him for taking care of the people nobody else would. I've seen him stand in the face of terrible opposition because he believed it was the right thing to do. Why is this so different?"

"It just is."

"That's no answer."

"It's the only one I have. Just give him time," she said as she hugged me.

But time is the one thing we didn't have.

BLAKE

SOMETIMES I THINK I'M invisible. That's the way it is with middle children anyway, but it's worse in my family. Hannah is the baby and the only girl—Daddy's girl—and Tyler has always got some drama going. So I have no idea where I fit in, or even if I fit at all.

I used to think life was perfect. Unlike Tyler, I had a pretty easy going relationship with Dad. We had so much in common. I even thought for a while that I'd go into ministry like him. But when I was old enough to see the toll it took on him, I knew it wasn't for me. Maybe that's when I first noticed that a distance had crept between us. Not a wide gulf, like the one that existed between him and Tyler, but it was still noticeable. Maybe it was because I was spending more time with my friends and my girlfriend, or maybe it was because he seemed more determined than ever to fight for the people who didn't have a voice, but we just didn't spend much time together anymore.

He had promised he'd help me practice for the driver's license test. For weeks I tried to schedule something. Either he was busy or I was. Mom took me a few times when Dad had to cancel. So I thought I was ready for the road test. I wasn't. When I stopped the car at the curb just minutes after I had headed out with the officer, Dad looked puzzled. The officer peeled a piece of paper off the pad and handed it to me. "You can try again in one week," he said as he got out of the car. I unbuckled before getting out and going around to the passenger side. Dad talked to the officer and then shook his hand and climbed into the car.

"It happens to the best of us," he said. He was smiling. I knew he was, even if I wasn't looking at him. For him, there was always a silver lining, always a lesson to be learned. Most of the time, I was okay with that, but not then. I was mad. Mad at him and mad at me. So I just crossed my arms and stared out the window. When we got home, I brushed past Dad on the way to my room.

Since I was invisible, I doubt he even noticed.

HANK

I SET UP MY temporary home behind an abandoned house by stringing up an old painter's tarp I'd found in the trash. I knew it was temporary because eventually someone would find me there and call the cops. Ever since the vagrancy laws were passed, people get uptight when one of us hangs around too long. So I never get too attached to any one place. Still I hoped this one would last longer because it felt secluded in the back corner of that lot—just the way I liked it. No one prying into my business or stealing my stuff—not that there's much to steal.

You don't choose to be homeless, at least not the first time. Maybe not even the second or third time. But when you spend the better part of your adult life in one make-shift home or another, you come to realize that it's a choice. Maybe not a conscious one, but one that's a result of all the other choices you made—and keep making—knowing full well that they'll only leave you without a home or family or friends.

There's a strange comfort, though, in knowing that there's nothing left to lose. I knew I could flip off the world and no one gave a damn. Except the reverend. Even when I couldn't hang onto my job after I left the halfway house and even after I lost the next job within six months, he was still there. No matter how fucked up I was, he kept showing up trying to pour hope back into my life. I guess he couldn't see the tiny holes filling my insides that kept letting the hope ooze back out. It wasn't really a surprise when he showed up on that summer afternoon, even though I'd gone out of my way to avoid him.

I'd been miserable for days as the temperatures and humidity climbed. The dog days of summer, I think they call it. I tried everything I could to find relief, including sneaking into that old house through a loose board in the back. But the heat just baked the mold and piss in that closed up space so that the smell was unbearable. So I ended up spending a lot of time under the shade of the trees and my make-shift tent and fanning myself every now and then with a piece of cardboard. That afternoon, I had fallen asleep stretched out on top of that old sleeping bag the reverend had given me.

I guess I was in a deep sleep because I didn't hear him come into the yard. It was the sound of an old can hitting against the broken concrete patio that woke me up.

"What the ----." I sprang to my feet. "Reverend, you scared the hell out of me."

"Sorry, man. I called your name a couple of times. You were sleeping pretty sound."

"Yeah, well I don't get much sleep at night."

"Still having those nightmares?"

"Sometimes." I really didn't want to talk about it. Actually I was tired of talking about it. I had been avoiding him for weeks so I wouldn't have to talk about it. "How the hell did you find me anyway?"

"Someone at the food pantry said they saw you in this area, so I thought I'd see if I could find you. I haven't seen you in a while and I was worried. You left the motel without saying a word and you stopped showing up at your job."

"Look, Reverend, I appreciate your concern, but I don't need a damn babysitter." It sounded ungrateful. It probably was. He had paid for the motel and had vouched for me so I could get that job at the hardware store. That's exactly the reason I'd been avoiding him. He'd want to know why I walked out on him and left my sobriety in the dust. It wasn't easy to explain. Hell, I'm not sure it made sense to me. I just know that one morning I looked in the mirror and didn't recognize the man looking back. He was clean shaven with hair that was washed and combed. But he wasn't real. I could see it in his eyes. They were hollow because the real man inside was hollow, completely empty. No heart, no passion, no soul. Those had been stripped from him years ago. So I left him, that phony plastic man, behind. Living on the streets is hard, but at least I know it's real. That I'm real.

"I'm not trying to babysit you, Hank. I just want to make sure you're okay, that's all. Especially in this heat. I brought you some water." He set down several bottles onto the sleeping bag.

"I'll never be okay. You should know that by now."

"I don't believe that."

"I don't care what the hell you believe. Just leave me alone." I expected him to go but he just stood there like a fucking idiot. "Didn't you hear me? I told you to get the fuck out of here." I shoved him and he stumbled backward but then caught his balance. He looked like a wounded bird, which made me hate him all the more. Just as he turned to go I heard several loud pops that sounded like gunfire.

"Get down, Robbie," I screamed as I pushed him to the ground and then threw myself on top of him. "Damn Viet Cong," I whispered. My heart was beating fast and I could barely catch my breath.

"It's okay, Hank. It's okay. We're in Mercy, remember? That was only some firecrackers. Somebody's just starting their Fourth of July celebrations a little early."

"Fourth of July?" I said. I looked down and saw the reverend staring wild-eyed at me. I raised up off him and fell back onto my ass. "I forgot it was the Fourth," I said, still a little dazed.

"Those fireworks will be going off all night," he said as he sat up. "Are you sure you're going to be all right?"

"No, but nothing's going to change that, is it? Just go." He stared at me, trying to see if I was serious, I guess. "Please go," I whispered. "Why don't you pretend I never existed. We'll both be happier if you do."

He shook his head but got up anyway to leave. Only when he reached the broken gate did he turn back for one final look before disappearing beyond the overgrown hedges. I sat there for a good long while. The sun was hanging low in the sky and it was hot as hell. Beads of sweat formed on my forehead and rolled down my back, but I didn't move. I kept thinking about Robbie. God, he was such a good kid. He could make me laugh until I snorted, which would make us both laugh that much harder.

He was so naive about the war. Hell, we both were. All through basic training and even through our first few days in country, we were having fun playing soldier in our olive-green field jackets and helmets. But then we saw old women and children and mothers clutching babies fleeing burned out villages. We saw the bodies of soldiers—theirs and ours—scattered around, turning green fields red. We saw things no human should ever see. We didn't talk about it. No words could ever capture the burden of those images. And even though we could see it in each other's eyes, we laughed our way through it. As if by instinct, we knew that our laughter was the only barrier between us and insanity.

But then Robbie died and there was nothing to keep me grounded.

My brother took me to DC several years ago to see the memorial. I searched the catalog at the end of the wall until I found his name, and then Doug helped me locate the right panel. There it was. *Robert J Webster*. I reached out and touched the letters etched into the stone like, if by magic, he would step out of that stone whole and laugh at my gullibility for believing he was dead. But he *was* dead. And his forever-youthful grin was forced to fade back into the haze of my memory. Doug helped me rub his name onto a paper, which I kept for a long time. I was upset when I lost it, but it was only a name on a paper. It would never ever be him.

Robbie would have liked the reverend, I thought. If things had been different, I could imagine the three of us sitting down with some beer and discussing the finer points of philosophy or debating the best kind of music. Robbie would be acting silly until he had me snorting and the reverend in tears because he was laughing so hard. But Robbie was gone and dredging up his ghost always took one more piece of me and left me gasping for air.

Finally, in the growing darkness, I crawled back to the shelter of the tarp. I hadn't eaten since early that morning, so I fumbled around in my backpack for the peanut butter and crackers I'd picked up from the food pantry. My hand felt the smooth whiskey bottle and lingered on it before finally moving on. *You need to eat,* I told myself. But the fireworks began popping all around me. Every whistling rocket, every loud explosion settled into my bones until I trembled with panic. I found the bottle again and took a big sip. I let the warmth of it fill the emptiness.

Before I drifted off to sleep, I was still thinking of Robbie but it was the reverend's face that came to me in my dreams.

FRED

WE WERE SUPPOSED TO meet at eight at the church so we could go to Colby's Pool Hall together, something we'd been doing once a month for a couple of years. It was a chance to play a little pool but mostly a chance to meet people and talk with them about their lives—offer prayer or assistance when we could, but definitely listen to their stories. I've learned that more times than not people just want somebody to listen to them. Grayson had to practically drag me there the first few times. He was more comfortable in those situations than I was. But I grew into it and began to look forward to it every month.

When I got to the church, I thought I had misunderstood the meeting arrangements because it looked like his office was dark. But then I noticed a dim light coming from his desk. He was bent over a piece of paper, deeply engrossed in whatever it was he was writing.

"Working late on your sermon?" I asked.

He looked up and stared at me for a minute before speaking. "Actually, it's a love letter," he said. Seeing my puzzled look, he added, "to Tyler."

I didn't have to ask what that was about. He and Tyler had had a rocky relationship for some time. Natalie had talked to Effie about Grayson's struggle with Tyler being gay, but Grayson and I had never talked about it, though I had considered bringing it up. I had that same struggle when our granddaughter came out, but I imagined it was more difficult for a father and his son. Anyway, I figured that Grayson would talk about it when he was ready. Now seemed to be the time.

"Tyler is gay," he said. "I see you're not surprised. I'm sure Natalie has told Effie." I nodded. "Ever since he hit his teens, we've butted heads. At first I thought it was typical teenage angst that was made even more intense by Tyler's headstrong personality. When he told me last year that he's gay, his moodiness began to make sense. But I haven't handled it well, even though I guess I suspected it for some time."

"It can be a shock to hear, even if you suspect it," I said.

"For a while, I think I was just grieving. All the dreams I had for him suddenly vanished—or at least it felt that way. No wife, and probably no children. But then the fear set in. I see what happens to gay men and it terrifies me."

The lines on his brow grew closer together. It was the same look he had when he dealt with Reed.

"I'm ashamed to admit that what I felt for a long time, and perhaps more intensely, was anger. What kept running through my head was how this was going to affect me. Ministry here has never been easy. God forgive me, but I was more concerned about what people would think of me than what Tyler was going through."

Even in the dim light, I saw the tear that slipped down his cheek. I thought about saying something—some word of comfort or encouragement—but he had been holding his own words for a while, so I just let them tumble out of him.

"I've been thinking about my own dad a lot lately. He was never good at expressing emotion, unless it was disapproval. I wonder when I became him."

"It's scary, isn't it? My father was a stern man, too. I told myself I'd never tell my children to straighten up and fly right and then one day, there I was with those words coming out of my mouth. I was sure my father was standing behind me but, no, it was me. I think they call that the transitive property of fathers."

Grayson laughed. "I want to leave a better legacy for my own children. I think I need to start with Tyler. All he wants from me is to acknowledge who he is—who he is completely. I'm hoping this letter is a beginning. Maybe it will begin to heal the wounds I've inflicted. And then I need to write one to Blake and Hannah, too. I want to be a better father."

"I don't guess you ever feel like the kind of father you want to be," I said. "I wonder if our fathers felt the same way?"

"Maybe," he said and smiled. "It would be nice to think so anyway. Dad would seem different to me if that was the case." He gathered some papers and a book into a pile and then stood up. "I guess we'd better get moving if we're going to go to Colby's."

Once we were in the car, the conversation quickly turned to the competition we usually had about who was the better billiards player. The truth is that Grayson usually beat the pants off me, but there was no fun in admitting he was better. That was one of the things I loved about our trips to Colby's—ribbing each other mercilessly. Our friendship had deepened in the last year. Maybe it was because we realized we had nearly lost it. Sometimes that gives you a sense of urgency to hold on to something tighter. Maybe it was because our relationship felt like the father and son relationship we wished we had had with our own fathers. Whatever it was, I treasured that one night every month with just Grayson and me.

My stomach did tighten, though, every time we drove to Colby's. The pool hall itself wasn't a bad place. Rick, the owner, always kept it clean, and he didn't tolerate raucous behavior. I'd seen him bounce a few people before, but most people just came in for a few beers and a game or two of pool. The area around Colby's, though, was a different story. It was in the area of town I didn't feel comfortable in during the daytime, so I was always anxious to come there after dark. Grayson, though, seemed to take it all in stride.

When we pulled into the parking lot at Colby's, which was full, Grayson commented that the odds were greater that we'd find someone in there who needed to tangibly see God's love. So we stepped out of the car with the anticipation of God showing up.

The air was thick with summer heat. It was a black night with the sliver of the moon sitting low in the sky. A single street light was well down the block, so the parking lot was dark except for the small circle of light just in front of the door and from the picture window. Music playing inside spilled into the parking lot as a couple came out the door, laughing and holding on to each other. They smelled of beer and cigarettes when they passed us as we came around Grayson's car, and we exchanged friendly greetings.

We were not far from the front door when I saw movement in the shadows, between two cars. And then I heard what sounded like a low growl. I jumped and turned toward the sound, ready to protect myself from an angry dog. I was on the ground before I knew it, pushed down with a force that knocked the wind out of me. From where I was laying I could see commotion a few feet away. I heard the animal-like growl again followed by a shriek. And then I saw a shadowy figure disappear through the cars.

I picked myself up and stumbled to a second shadowy figure still laying on the ground. It was Grayson, moaning softly. Even with the muffled music pulsing behind me, coming from Colby's, I could hear the gurgle in Grayson's throat. I bent over him and called his name but he said nothing in response. When I touched his chest, I felt the warm wetness on his shirt.

The door to Colby's opened and a man came out.

"He's been hurt," I screamed. "Somebody call an ambulance!"

Even then, I knew it was too late.

BLESSED ARE THOSE WHO MOURN

RICK

HE WAS A REGULAR at Colby's, certainly ever since I've owned it. They both were, actually. Grayson came in at least once a month, almost without fail. I never imagined in a million years that it would end like this. That's the kind of thing that happens in big cities, not in Mercy.

I liked Grayson right from the start. He didn't let on at first that he was a preacher, not that it would have really mattered to me. He told me one time, though, that he didn't like people to know he was a preacher. "It changes the way they are around me," he said. "They're either judging the things I do or say or they think I'm judging them. Sometimes I just like to be Grayson."

"Well, if you need a place to just be Grayson, you're always welcome here."

Even when he came in with Fred, he rarely did the preacher thing. They just played billiards and talked to people. Sometimes I'd see him praying with people, not that you could tell it by watching him. He just looked like he was talking with them, but they'd have their heads bowed. "People have a hard time getting past traditions," he said to me once. I guess I was one of them, because it did seem strange to me at first. My mother would have tanned my hide if I didn't bow my head and close my eyes during mealtime prayers. It was disrespectful to do that, she said.

"I try never to contradict someone's mother. That gets me in trouble," he said with a laugh when I told him this once. "But I suspect God is more concerned with the condition of our hearts than the position of our heads." Some people would have been insulted by that, but I smiled when Grayson said it. It's what I wished I'd said myself. It was the way I had always pictured God.

Grayson was one of the good ones. I can't believe that I won't ever see him again.

Hank was a different story altogether. It's not that he's bad, but he certainly has his demons. He was in here that night, drinking heavy like he often does. After a while, he started ranting, shouting so loud that he could be heard above the music and the clinking of billiard balls. It's not like he was making any sense either. He rarely does. I finally had to tell him to leave.

I wish I hadn't. Grayson would probably still be alive.

HANK

I DON'T REMEMBER MUCH. Only disembodied voices. I lay them out in my mind, side by side, trying to splice together something that makes sense. But it doesn't. It always stops short of an ending, certainly not the ending they tell me really happened. *Maybe that's a blessing,* I keep telling myself. *Maybe I can create a new ending. A different ending.*

Of course I've never been able to change a damn thing in this life. I don't know what makes me think I can change this. So I'm stuck reliving it in slow motion.

The scene starts out clear. The mustard yellow walls of Colby's Pool Hall are lined with photographs of all the greats. Willie Mosconi, Earl Strickland, Buddy Hall, Minnesota Fats. The two billiards tables are on the far side, away from the door and the bar. Three silver lights hang low over each table. Music is blaring loudly through the speakers in the corner, usually some rocking country tunes. Some nights there are even girls in short shorts and cowboy hats trying to do line dances on the small dance floor.

It's a familiar sight to me. I like going there because I can usually hustle drinks. I'm a fair pool player—one of the few skills I've been able to refine over the years. I was on fire that night. It was like I couldn't lose, so the beer and whiskey was flowing freely for me. It didn't take long for me to start feeling the buzz. And then came the loud talking. That's when I always get myself into trouble—by talking smack. Some guy was giving it right back. Not sure exactly what he said. Hell, I don't remember what I said, but I wasn't going to let that little piss talk to me like that. I tried to yell above the music but it was loud. So I kept yelling louder. When someone stepped in front of me, I tried to swing my fist at him but I stumbled forward and landed hard on the floor. There was laughter, I think, though I can't be certain. That music was too damn loud.

The guy that runs the place came over and looked down at me. "It's time for you to leave," he yelled down at me. And then he kicked me in the small of my back. I heaved myself up on all fours, while the floor seemed to be tilting from side to side, like one of those labyrinth games where you try to avoid dropping the ball in holes along the way. I staggered to the door and flung myself outside or…was I pushed out. I don't remember.

It was dark and hot. God, it was hot. I stumbled between a couple of cars before falling to the ground again, crouching in the threatening blackness. The enemy was all around me, the hot breath on my neck. I heard the gunfire, at least I thought I did. Probably a car backfiring or something. It's happened before. I crouched lower, ready for the attack. From there, it's only blackness. Only fragments. Splicing together the fragments.

Music—muted and then loud and then muted again.

Melting into the blackness.

Laughter—flirty and taunting.

Voices. What are they saying? I can't hear what they're saying. Is that growling? Where is it coming from? From me? Is it coming from me?

Shadows moving. Coming toward me. They are the enemy. They must be stopped.

Blue lights pulsing into the blackness. Separating darkness into light. And then blackness. Nothing but blackness…until the bright lights of the jail start bringing me back to myself. Until the blood on my hands becomes an unwelcome memorial. I don't want to remember. Not this. Not the final meeting. I'll only remember the first meeting. The beginning cannot be the ending. So that's what I'll remember. I'll remember the beginning.

FRED

The officer stood in front of me asking questions, but my eyes were locked on the stretcher being loaded into the ambulance. I caught a glimpse of Grayson's face, which was ghostly amid the flashes of red and blue lights. It was all too real, and yet, the images play in my mind like a scene in a stylized movie, cutting from image to image without connective tissue. Sometimes circling—catching every angle in excruciating detail. Despite the blackness of the night, my mind captures it all, filling in the missing elements that must have been.

The paramedics and police arrive at the same time. Someone is dragging me away from Grayson. I don't know who it is, but I fight them. I can't leave Grayson's side. Even though it doesn't make sense, my mind tells me that if I let them take him, then it's the same as admitting that it's over. I'm not ready for it to be over. The officer grabs me by the shoulders and says something, but nothing is registering in my mind. The words sound strange, like they're coming out in slow motion. I look over the policeman's shoulder and see the stretcher being loaded into the ambulance.

"I need you to tell me what happened," the officer is saying. The doors to the ambulance slam shut, and I try to muscle my way toward them, but the officer holds me back. "They've got to take him now. But I need you to tell me what happened. It will be okay."

But it isn't okay. We both know it.

I look at the officer, his face glowing blue. "He came out of nowhere," I say. My voice is flat. Whatever emotion might have been there left with the ambulance. "He knocked me down and then jumped on Grayson. He might have said something. I don't know. It all happened so fast."

"But you didn't see him—the man who attacked you?"

"Not really. I got a quick look at his face. He looked familiar, but it was so dark."

"Hey, over here. I found this," another officer said, holding up a knife that also glistened blue in the flashing lights.

"My friend," I say. I don't want the officer to be distracted. "I have to be with my friend. I have to call my wife. Oh my God. I have to call his wife." My mind is racing. Too many thoughts to process at once.

"It's okay," the officer says as he touches my arm. "We'll get someone to drive you to the hospital. We can finish up later—and we already have an officer on his way to the Armstrong's house."

I nod, as if I understand. But I don't understand any of it.

"We've got someone," an officer yells from the blackness. "I think he's passed out." Two officers rush into the darkness while another helps me into the front seat of his cruiser. As the police car drives away with me inside, I see the people gathered outside the door. They are clinging to each other, silhouettes against the bright light streaming from Colby's. Even though the scene is surreal, I'm plunged back into real time. My head drops back on the seat. More than any other time in my life, I want to feel God's presence. I want his spirit to rush over me like a mighty wind. Instead, I am swept back to a moment on top of a mountain with Grayson at least ten years before.

He had convinced me to go hiking, something I hadn't done since I was a teenager. But as usual Grayson had a way of getting me to do things I never thought I would. He told me it wasn't a difficult hike, and maybe for him it wasn't. But a little more than halfway up the trail, I wasn't sure I could make it.

"You can do it," he said when we stopped for me to catch my breath. "It's only a little farther. Trust me, it's worth it."

I nodded, not able to speak right away. I took a couple of deep breaths and then signaled that I was ready to start up the path again. The leaves, which had begun to fall, crunched beneath my feet. The cool autumn air felt good on my face. If nothing else, it was invigorating to watch Grayson in front of me bound over roots and up rocky ledges, stopping occasionally to make sure I was still following. I'd motion for him to go on, not wanting him to think

I wasn't able to keep up, even though I had nearly thirty years on him and probably thirty pounds, too.

Just when I thought I couldn't go anymore, the trail gave way to a clearing at the top of a ridgeline. A valley stretched in front of us in a patchwork of yellows, oranges, and reds, and another mountain rose on the other side of the valley, its sheer rock face towering toward the sky.

"This sure would make a body believe in God if they didn't already," I said.

"I know," Grayson said. "There is nowhere I feel closer to God than up on a mountain. Throw in the autumn colors, and his majesty is enough to make a grown man weep."

"I'm glad you said that," I laughed. "Now I don't feel so bad about wanting to cry." Grayson laughed, too, and lowered his backpack to the ground. Everything around us was still, even the trees. One of the trees near us had already shed its leaves except for a few obstinate ones that refused to give in to the inevitable.

"Be still and know that I am God," Grayson whispered. We stood silently for a while. And then, from deep in the valley, a rustling sound began moving up the mountain. Slowly, the trees below us began to shake with the gentle wind until it moved just over us. We both looked up at those five solitary leaves as they fluttered with the wind making two of them let go and fall to the forest floor. "That's just the way it is with the spirit of God," Grayson said, speaking to the wind. "Sometimes he comes so gently and if we're still, we can hear his presence before we feel it. And then we just have to let go and let him do the rest."

In all the time I had known him, Grayson was always the leaf that surrendered to the will of the spirit. But instinctively, I think, I clung to what felt safe. I was the leaf that stubbornly held on to the branch. Or at least I was back then. It had been easy to cling to the way it had always been. Not that God never moved in that old church or that I myself had never felt the spirit, but I had always been comfortable believing that the spirit kept me safely inside the walls of the church—away from the secular, evil world.

If God wanted anything done, he was going to have to bring it to me within the safety of the church. The truth is, I had spent years playing church—faithfully attending every Sunday and Wednesday night, faithfully serving as a Sunday School teacher and deacon, faithfully doing anything that was asked of me as long as it kept me comfortably inside the church. But then Grayson came and within a couple of months I found myself in that old factory talking with homeless men while never taking my hand off the rock in my pocket. For a long time, no matter how often Grayson talked me into doing something like going out to take care of the homeless, or no matter how much I agreed that it was what we *should* be doing, my stomach still got tied in knots. I wondered when—or if—I'd ever be comfortable following Grayson outside the walls of the church.

"It's good to be uncomfortable," Grayson said when I tried to explain my unease once. "That discomfort means that you are allowing God to use you as his hands and feet—and, more importantly, his heart. We like to think of the church as God's house, and that's all well and good. But the truth is, he doesn't live there. He lives out here, where people are—where they are searching for his light in the darkness. We have to be that light."

He was right, of course. But as the police car pulled into the emergency entrance of the hospital and I saw Natalie wrapped in Effie's arms, the world felt very dark indeed. Yet even as I wondered if we would ever find the light again, I also knew that we would never be comfortable if we didn't go out into the world searching for it—and that's just the way Grayson would have wanted it.

REED

I SAT BY MISS Addie's bed and watched her sleep. For weeks, she'd been sleeping most of the time, which the doctor said was normal. It was only a matter of time, he said—hours, maybe days. On one of the days when she was alert for a time, she told me that she had lived a good, long life so I was not to be sad. I tried to obey, but Addie had been like a mother to me, especially after my own mother passed. So even though she was ninety-one, letting go of Addie was still difficult, probably because it brought with it memories of being at the bedside of my mother as she breathed her last breath.

Addie was alone, except for me. She had lost Ollie years before, and their only child Mavis, who was just a couple of years older than me, passed away unexpectedly two years ago. It just about broke Addie's heart. "A parent isn't supposed to outlive her child," she said. But Addie had outlived everyone else that was close to her—two brothers and a sister, a handful of cousins, and two nieces. Her three nephews lived on the other side of the country, and only one actually ever checked on her. So it was up to me to take care of her. I would have done it for my mother's sake anyway, but I loved Miss Addie and wouldn't have been anywhere else but beside her bed.

She stirred a little, and I put my hand on her bony, cool hand. "It's okay, Miss Addie," I said. "I'm here." She quieted down again but I kept my hand on hers. I studied her face. Her bluish gray hair, not pinned up as usual, was splayed out behind her almost like a halo. Her cheeks were deeply lined but still full, and there was a hint of a smile on her lips. That was so typical of Addie, always with a smile.

I knew why Mom had loved Addie. She was such a gentle woman. They both were. Maybe that's why I was surprised by our final conversation a few days before.

"I guess I'll be putting the last cake in the oven soon," she said. Her soft voice had developed a raspy edge as she had aged.

"You've made some mighty fine cakes over the years. You know what my favorite was, don't you?" I smiled like I was six again.

"That's not hard. I've never seen anyone scarf down jam cake like you did."

"Only yours, Miss Addie. Only yours. Mom tried to make it a couple of times, but it never came out the same."

She sighed. "Your mama was a saint. She was taken too soon. I often wonder if it was from a broken heart."

"Because of losing my father?"

"Because of your father period." Her voice was mysterious. Mom and Dad weren't very affectionate with each other but I'd never witnessed any outright hostility. Addie looked at me and her pale blue eyes watered. "Your mama loved him—worshipped him was more like it. I guess your father couldn't handle a love that intense. At least that's the only reason I can think of for him stepping out on her."

My chest tightened. Mom had never let on that Dad had cheated on her. Even on her deathbed, she never uttered a word against him. I wasn't sure why Addie was telling me this now.

"I don't mean to upset you, but something told me that you needed to know. Not because of what you father did, but because of what your mama did. She forgave him. It wasn't easy, I can tell you that. There was many a night she cried at my kitchen table trying to find the strength to do it. Despite what he did, she still loved him, and she believed in reconciliation. *If I believe in God, how can I not believe in reconciliation,* she told me more than once. I don't know if she was trying to convince me or herself. But she never gave up on the promise of reconciliation. That's why she was a saint, Reed." Her eyes were piercing, more alert than they had been in weeks. "She chose forgiveness—even when he did it again…and again."

I sat quietly looking at Addie and then down at the floor. We had never talked this candidly before. She let me process the thought, let me try to comprehend the love and forgiveness as well as the betrayal and hurt. My father had been my hero when I was very young, but as I got older he became distant. Now I understood that the distance was about betrayal and not about me—or least not directly me.

"Why did she forgive him if he kept cheating on her?"

"She was a woman of faith, and that faith told her to forgive him."

"But scripture condemns adultery. She didn't have to stay with him and she certainly didn't have to forgive him."

"There's where you're wrong, honey. She stayed with him because she loved him. It may have been a foolish choice, but she made it with open eyes and an open heart. Forgiveness, though, is another matter altogether. Forgiveness is about finding peace inside yourself. Your mother knew that. She may have died of a broken heart, but she died knowing a peace that passes all understanding. I want you to have that peace, too."

"Me? I don't really understand."

"I think you need to find peace with Brother Armstrong." Grayson's name came out of nowhere and shook me in a way that even the news about my father hadn't. By way of explanation, she added, "He came by to see me a few days ago. We had a nice visit."

"Did he apologize to you for what he did to you and Ollie?"

"Not in so many words."

"I'm not surprised." I didn't try to hide my feelings. I was tired of talking about Grayson, even with Miss Addie.

"That's what I mean, sweetie," she said. "I can hear the bitterness in your voice. Maybe it's time to find the peace that will come with forgiving him. I have."

Addie meant well, so I suppressed the anger that was bubbling up. He might have put her up to it, but even if he hadn't he probably had ulterior motives. Knowing Grayson, it was probably somehow all about him. He was an arrogant S.O.B, pardon my language. But it's the truth. He thought he knew it all and wasn't about to listen to anyone else. God knows I tried to tell him his ways wouldn't work, not here in Mercy. Maybe not anywhere. But it had to be his way or the highway—like God spoke only to him. I couldn't forgive him, not even for Miss Addie.

She realized that without me saying anything—probably because I didn't say anything—so we talked about Ollie instead. She told one story after another and I laughed until I cried. It was a good way to remember both of them.

Despite the strangeness of that last conversation, I wished I could hear her one more time as I watched her breathing grow more shallow. But I knew she was ready to see Ollie and Mavis and Mom again. At one point, she opened her eyes and reached out for something even though nothing was there. She was looking intently at whatever it was, and I thought I saw a faint smile on her face. I'd like to think it was one of them she saw, maybe all three, waiting for her.

When she was finally released from this world, I bent my head against her frail hand and wept. She was the last thread that connected me to the old ways. I thought about what she had told me about my father's betrayal. It gnawed at me. Not just what he did but that he got away with it. He took advantage of Mom's love and by doing so, he never got what he deserved. I had never made a connection between my dad and Grayson, but Addie's talk made me knit the two of them together in my mind. At the core they were more alike than I realized. They had a cavalier attitude about betrayal and an indifference about its impact on others.

For years I had watched Grayson destroy everything and everyone in his path. There never seemed to be any real consequence to his actions. I wish I could have found the peace that Addie and Mom found in forgiveness, but I couldn't shake the desire that maybe one day Grayson, even if my Dad hadn't, would get what he deserved.

I guess that day was yesterday. It's not that I wanted Grayson dead—not really. But in all honesty, I can't say that I'm sorry it happened to him the way it did. He was hoisted with his own petard by Hank, the guy Grayson adopted as his pet project, all while tearing the church apart. Poetic justice, if you ask me.

So if you're waiting for me to say that I'm sorry he got what he deserved, well, you'll be waiting a long time. If that sounds cold, well maybe it is. But I don't have time to feel sorry for him. I'll tell you who I'm sorry for. Addie and Ollie. I'm even sorry for Natalie and her children. But I've been sorry for them—and this whole community—for a very long time.

JAMAL

He believed in justice. He didn't care who you were or where you came from, he stood up for people, particularly those people who didn't have a voice. Maybe the most important thing he did was listen. He heard our stories, educated himself on our pain. He stood beside us, and when it was necessary, he stood for us. It's hard to find that in this world, but especially in this small town. I was glad to call him friend.

EFFIE

When Fred called, the panic in his voice gave me goose bumps. In all the time we've been married, I have never heard him like that. He was breathless, like he was drowning, struggling to get enough air to say words. But the words weren't making any sense. I finally got enough out of him to realize that something had happened to Grayson and that I needed to get to the hospital immediately. So I grabbed my keys and rushed out the door.

The ambulance, with its lights still flashing, was in front of the emergency room door when I arrived at the hospital. The back doors were open and I could see it was empty. When I walked to the other side of the ambulance, I saw Karen Newsom standing beside it in her paramedic uniform. Karen's a member at Ignite who I know very well. She wasn't supposed to tell me anything, but I could see by the look on her face that it wasn't good. She just shook her head. I felt lightheaded and stumbled back against the ambulance. She caught me and helped me to a nearby bench. She made sure I was all right, and when her partner came out of the emergency room, they closed the ambulance doors and left.

I was alone.

For a moment, it was quiet except for a cricket chirping in the bushes behind the bench. But my thoughts were not quiet. They raced around in a hazy mess as I tried to comprehend a world without Grayson. I was trying to sort them out when a police car pulled up. The officer stepped out and walked around to open the passenger door. When Natalie emerged, the officer had to hold her arm to steady her. I ran to her side and our eyes locked.

"He's gone," I whispered.

"You're lying," she whispered back, not as an accusation but more like a plea. Her knees gave way. She would have slid to the ground if the officer and I weren't holding on to her.

"I'm sorry, Mrs. Armstrong," the officer said.

"Thank you," she said. The words came out, but her face was blank. I nodded a thank you to the officer as he got back in his car and then I helped Natalie to the sidewalk.

"Effie," she said, staring helplessly into my eyes. It was a question as much as a statement, loaded with the *how's* and *why's* she could not yet speak. I folded her into my arms and held her tight. We stood that way for a time, until Fred came up followed by another officer.

"Oh, Fred," Natalie whispered as she put her arms around him. He hugged her right back, even though he is not usually comfortable in those situations.

"I'm so sorry," he whispered back to her.

Together we went in the emergency room. A doctor came out and took us to a small consultation room. His voice was low and sounded like the hum of a machine. I wondered how many times he had had to tell families what they didn't want to hear. He tried to prepare us for seeing Grayson, though that seemed impossible, and then he led us back to the room where Grayson was.

The bed was in the center of the small room and the floor surrounding it was dotted with red-stained gauze. In the dim light, it took a moment to see the body, covered to the neck by a white sheet. Seeing that it was really him, Natalie gasped and turned her head. She clutched my arm as if she was trying to draw strength from me, but she wasn't going to find it because I felt like I might pass out, too. We walked to where Grayson lay, me and Natalie on one side of the bed and Fred on the other.

Grayson's face was strangely serene, but then what other way would he look? His life had been a monument to blessedness.

Natalie reached down to touch his face, her hand trembling. She stroked his cheek and smoothed back his hair. Her motion was slow and deliberate, never taking her eyes off of his face. At one point, her knees buckled again, and I motioned for Fred to get her a chair. But when he brought it to her, she refused to sit. She stayed with him for a while, stroking his face, stopping only occasionally to wipe her own cheek.

"We probably need to get you back home, sweetie," I finally said to her, not wanting to rip her away but also knowing that prolonging the leaving would not bring about his staying with us. I put my arm gently around her shoulder. She jerked away from me, not with anger but with pleading in her eyes. Mine could only answer back with helplessness. I didn't know what else to do. She looked back at Grayson.

"I love you," she said—as clear and firm as she had said anything that night. "I will always love you."

She gave me her hand and I gently turned her toward the door. Her feet moved like they were weighted with blocks of lead, but mine weren't any better. At the door, she turned for a final look. She held onto the door frame so tightly that her fingers turned white.

While Fred was helping Natalie into the front seat of our car, I called Tyler to let him know we were coming home. His voice carried little emotion. Perhaps it was shock, but since his relationship with Grayson had been so tenuous, I couldn't be sure.

Fred seemed to be driving rather slow. I suppose his mind was distracted, but it could have easily been me. Everything seemed to be happening in slow motion. As we passed under a street light, I saw Fred looking at me in the rear view mirror. My focus had been so much on Grayson and Natalie that I hadn't even paused long enough to realize that it could have been Fred, too. I quickly looked away to try to align my heart rate with the slow motion movement of the car.

The boys greeted us at the door when we got to the house. Natalie's tears up to now had only come slowly and quietly. Suddenly she began to cry in great, heaving sobs. Blake and Tyler enveloped her in a huddle and held her until the sobs slowed, and then they walked her to the couch.

"Here, honey," I said as I handed her a glass of water and a pill.

"What's that?" she asked.

"It's something to help you sleep. The doctor sent it home."

She looked at me with her red, puffy eyes. "I can't sleep. What about my children? What about Hannah? My children need me."

"Of course they do. Tyler and I will watch after everyone. You've got some difficult days ahead and you must get some rest. I promise I'll stay as long as I'm needed."

"It's okay, Mom," Tyler said, and Blake nodded. She looked at me again and nodded, although it seemed to only be an echo of theirs. I escorted her upstairs and helped her into bed, not even bothering to change her clothes. She tried to speak, but I quieted her and pulled the covers up over her before turning off the light. When I came back downstairs, Blake had gone up to his room but Fred and Tyler were talking.

"So they got the guy that did this?" Tyler said.

"I think so," Fred said. "They seemed to have found someone just as I left for the hospital."

I sat down next to Fred and slipped my hand into his. He glanced at me and smiled—the first time any of us smiled that night. It faded quickly as we all returned to the solemn reality.

"It's been a difficult night for the two of you," Tyler said. "You should go home and get some sleep."

"Fred can go home," I said looking at Fred, nodding at him with approving eyes. And then I turned back to Tyler. "I promised your mother I would stay."

"I appreciate the offer, Effie, but we'll be okay. You can come back in the morning, if you like. I know Mom would appreciate it."

As I listened to his words and noticed the confidence in the way he leaned forward and took my hand, I realized that a man sat in front of me—a man Grayson would be proud of. I squeezed Tyler's hand and promised I would be back in the morning.

A light rain had begun to fall by the time we left the house. The steady swish of the wipers made me sleepy. I was ready to lay my head on a pillow and hope sleep would come, but at the same time, I dreaded sleep, or at least what dreams may come. I couldn't bear for Grayson to be confined now only to my dreams. The thought of it brought the tears that I had been guarding until such a moment. Fred reached over and placed his hand on my knee. His warm flesh against mine was a reminder that no matter how far away it seemed, comfort would be found.

FLORENCE

I'M SORRY THAT HAPPENED to him, but he never had respect for us. He came to this town with his big city ideas and big city values. Grayson showed no respect for our traditions or values. It was like we were a bunch of backward yokels who needed to be civilized and taught the "right" way to do everything.

Well, I guess if he wanted big city life in this small town, he sure got a taste of it in the very end.

DALTON

His self-righteous crusading nearly cost me my business—or at least made it harder for me. Those church people are always trying to shut me down. Mostly they file complaints to the city, but I've always been able to stop them before they get very far. We bring in money to the city, after all. The mayor and the City Council may not like us, but they can't afford to shut us down.

But that Armstrong guy, he'd come in every once in a while and drink with the patrons—buddy up with them. And then he'd talk with the dancers on their breaks. Tell them there was a better life for them. He'd even offer them assistance. I had more than one of them quit on me because of him. Not that it did much good. Several of them came crawling back and those that didn't, I could easily replace. So as far as I was concerned, he was just like all the rest of those religious snobs, and I could do without the whole lot of them.

TYLER

THE SKY WAS A brilliant pink, casting everything on the back porch with a rosy glow. On any other morning, such a sunrise would have anticipated a beautiful day, but the day ahead promised to be anything but beautiful. As I sipped my coffee and stared into the pink sky, I tried to clear my mind. It felt like a dream—the officer at the door, his solemn words, Mom's knees buckling and her sliding to the floor, the officer helping her to the car to take her to the hospital. "Watch after your brother and sister," she said to me as she climbed into the car. When Effie called from the hospital later, her words were simple. "He's gone."

He's gone, I repeated to the pink sky. *How could this happen?* There was no answer, and there would be none. How could meaning be made out of something so senseless? But Dad would have somehow found the meaning.

I took another sip of coffee. The sliding door opened and Mom emerged. She was still in her clothes from the night before and her blond hair was tousled. She scooted back one of the wrought iron chairs and sank onto it.

"Are you okay?" I said, knowing that it was probably the most foolish question I could have asked.

"No." Her voice was deflated but strangely calm. She stared at me, but it was like she was looking through me. "I don't think I'll ever be okay again," she whispered.

"Did you sleep at all?"

"I guess so. It doesn't feel like I did." She drew her knees to her chest, and for a minute, she looked like a little girl, except for the lines in her forehead. "Did Effie leave?" she asked.

"Yeah, she left soon after you went upstairs. She didn't want to go, but I told her we'd be all right. I think she'll be coming back over this morning." I paused. "Mark is coming this morning, too."

"Mark?" She looked confused.

"I told you about him the other day. I hope it's okay for him to come."

She nodded. "Of course," she said, but I wasn't sure she understood.

I needed Mark and was so glad he said he was coming. He didn't even give me the chance to ask. "I'll be there in the morning," he had said as soon as I told him what had happened. "I can come right now if you need me to." Knowing how comforting it was to have Mark on his way made me understand a little more what Mom must have been feeling knowing that Dad could not be there to comfort her—would never be there to comfort her again.

"I don't want to rush you," I said to her, "but we need to think about the service."

"I know," she said. "I've been thinking about it all night. It feels like a dream—maybe it really was in a dream—but I think your father has already said the words that need to heard at the service. He has pages and pages of sermon notes in his office. Would you be willing to go there and find something that feels right?"

"Sure," I said. Going through Dad's office was really the last thing I wanted to do, but I knew Mom was not up to it.

"Hannah will be up soon," she said looking up toward Hannah's window. "How on earth do I tell her?"

That's how it was going to be for a while, I thought. The pain of telling people and people expressing their pain. Blake and I had already experienced it—hearing the words and processing what they meant. Holding each other in an awkward silence. Me trying to comfort his tears while trying to wrestle with my own lack of them. The two of us holding Mom when she and Effie came back from the hospital. Her tears wetting my shirt as I held her tight. Maybe I was a coward, but I couldn't face Hannah. I couldn't bear to see her bright eyes fill with tears when she learned that Dad would never be coming home. Would she even understand, I wondered. So when Blake showed up on the patio rubbing the sleep from his eyes, I excused myself to take a shower.

As the hot water flowed over me and the steam billowed above the shower curtain, my mind filled with my last conversation with Dad. Not the mechanical *how was your day* kind of conversations that often happened at dinner, but the deeper kind that happened too rarely between us. It was a few days before the confrontation about Mark, which I don't consider a conversation at all.

We were home alone, a rarity in this Grand Central Station of a house. He was fixing a sandwich when I came into the kitchen. I walked up beside him and got out a couple of slices of bread. We just went about making our sandwiches with neither of us saying anything at first. And then he asked if I wanted chips and I uttered a thank you. We were on course for our normal surface-level conversation, so I sat down at the kitchen table and began reading.

"What's that?" Dad asked, nodding toward the book.

"Oh, it's a biography of Dietrich Bonhoeffer. One of my professors suggested it. I'm almost finished."

"Bonhoeffer's life is fascinating, isn't it?"

I nodded and started to go back to reading, but I closed the book instead.

"Is something wrong?" he asked.

"I was just wondering if you'd ever realized that something you believed to be true was all wrong?"

"Oh my, yes," he said. His eyes lit up, like he'd opened a secret box with a hidden treasure. "Sometimes I think my whole spiritual journey has been nothing but sharp turns. Every time I think I have something figured out, God shows me where I took a wrong step, and then I'm off in a different direction."

"Is that what keeps getting you into trouble at church?"

"What makes you think I get into trouble?" He smiled. "Seriously, that's why I admire people like Bonhoeffer. It takes courage to change the way you believe and even greater courage to stand against people who don't understand the change or why you've made it. And to take action in support of your new belief, well, that's where the real courage comes in. There can be a real heavy price for it."

"I guess you know something about heavy prices. I'm not sure I'd ever have that kind of courage," I said.

"Don't sell yourself short, Tyler," he said tapping my hand. "I've seen plenty of courage in you over the years. When the time comes for you to need the heavy duty courage, I have no doubt that you'll stand up for what's right." It was one of the few times that he praised me for anything, at least that I could remember. But then a few days later, we were right back where we had always been—at odds over who I am and his obvious discomfort with it.

That contrast was still on my mind when I went to Dad's office for the sermon notes. Mark had arrived, and I was grateful he could go with me because it was unsettling to walk into Dad's office knowing that it would soon be emptied of everything that was him. His guitar, his trophies, his books, the family photos.

"Aww, look at that," Mark said pointing to a picture. "Is that you?"

"Yeah." The photograph, which was on Dad's desk, was just me and him. I was very little, maybe two, and I was on his shoulders. We stood in front of a large sand castle on a beach somewhere. I had no memory of the moment, but I was struck by how happy we looked. We had been happy once. He had been happy with me, maybe because at that moment I was who he expected me to be.

"We'd better see if we can find those sermon notes," I said, anxious to turn my attention away from the reminder of how broken our relationship had become. I sat down at his desk and turned on his computer. As it was warming up, I noticed a book on top of some papers. It was Bonhoeffer's *The Cost of Discipleship.* A few pages were dog-eared and I turned to them. Among the highlighted passages, was the line, "When Christ calls a man, he bids him come and die." Dad must have underlined that passage years before. How prophetic it seemed now.

I laid the book down and then noticed that it had been covering a piece of paper that started with the heading "Dear Tyler." My chest tightened as I wondered if I should read what it said.

"What is it?" Mark asked.

"I don't know. I think it may be a letter to me, but I'm not sure I can read it—or even if I should."

"I think you have to. It's basically the last thing he'll ever say to you."

He was right, but that thought raised my apprehension even more. My hands trembled as I pulled the paper from beneath the book. Mark sat down across from me as I read the letter to myself.

Dear Tyler,

I can only begin this letter by saying I love you. I love the man you are—who you are completely. I've failed you by not saying that to you, but more importantly, by not showing it to you. For that, I can only hope you'll forgive me.

After we talked the other day about Dietrich Bonhoeffer, I was reminded what he wrote. "By judging others we blind ourselves to our own evil and to the grace which others are just as entitled to as we are." Without really meaning to, I've failed to extend that grace to you. I've been blind to my own evil. Blind to my selfish desire to preserve what I've built. Blind to my arrogance that I was even the one who built it. Whatever you are and whatever you will become is because you are the child of grace-filled heavenly father not because you are the child of this selfishly blind father.

I hope we can

The letter stopped there, right in mid-sentence, like he had been interrupted. I stared at the words, trying to will them to completion. But there was just barren white space where words should have been.

RAMIE

DADDY'S GUITAR SAT IN the corner of the room, untouched. I couldn't bring myself to pick it up, not since I'd heard the news about Grayson. Music lost any comfort it usually brought, even though I wanted to feel close to Daddy and Grayson. Instead I just felt empty. So I wandered from room to room trying to find peace or comfort, but there wasn't any. There wasn't any at work, either.

The diner was busier for lunch than usual the day after it happened. The only topic anyone wanted to talk about was the incident at Colby's. Most people were shocked that something like that would happen in Mercy and to someone as good as Grayson. I heard a few spiteful comments, too, but I ignored them. Someone told me that it was Hank that did it. I didn't believe it at first. Hank had gotten into a few fist fights before, but I never thought of him being capable of stabbing someone—and not just anyone. It was Grayson, for Christ's sake. From the first time I saw them together, over in the corner booth, they had a bond. It wasn't just on Grayson's part, either. Hank took to Grayson like I've never seen him take to anyone else. If Hank did this, something must have happened.

Knowing that it was Hank left me unsettled. I had begun to see him through Grayson's eyes. Instead of seeing the town drunk or the freeloader always out for a handout, I saw the pain that was too reminiscent of my own. I felt like I was mourning Hank as well as Grayson. But while Hank's fate was still undetermined, Grayson's was all too real—and that meant a final farewell.

The visitation and service were scheduled at the church. I wondered if I should go to the visitation, if I would be welcome there. Not that I thought anyone would be hateful or turn me away, but I didn't really know anybody that would be there. As a pastor in the community, though, he almost certainly knew many people that his family and friends didn't know. Some of them were sure to be there, too. If I was being honest with myself, though, my reservations about going had more to do with facing my own grief. My heart tried to tell my head that if I didn't see him laying in a coffin then he wasn't really gone.

But as I was wrestling with the decision, I thought about what Grayson would have said to me. He would have laughed—that deep belly laugh that set him apart from all the other preachers I had known—and told me it was the only way he could think of to get me back in the church. I smiled at the thought of it, but it made the ache in my heart move even deeper.

The line for the visitation started forming even before the official time for it to start. I watched from the diner window as it steadily grew. *Maybe it will be shorter by the time I go home, get changed, and get back*, I thought. If anything, though, it was longer when I returned, even after I'd spent a good thirty minutes trying to decide what to wear.

I imagine Grayson would have been pleased by the variety of people who stood in line with me. We were an odd group. Elderly women in somber dresses and pearls. Young men in jeans and T-shirts sporting images that were a bit off color. Older men in coats and ties. Young women in brightly colored sundresses and flip flops. Mechanics just getting off work in their blue shirts with their names embroidered on a patch above the shirt pocket. Whatever our differences may have been on the surface, we were united in our grief. Even the burliest of men had to wipe away a tear as we waited to get into the church.

Once inside the building, I signed the guestbook just outside the doors into the main room. The line continued into the room, hovering around the edge as it wound its way to Grayson's family. I kept my gaze focused on them because I knew I wasn't prepared to see him yet. His wife greeted people warmly in her summery black slacks and white and black paisley shirt. A tissue was tucked in the palm of her hand and occasionally she used it to gently—gracefully—wipe a tear from her eye or cheek. She must have been exhausted, but the only sign of that was when one of her boys periodically put his arm around her shoulder or waist, as if to support her.

But it was Grayson's little girl that caught my attention. Her long blond her was pulled back by two pink bows and she wore a black and white polka dot dress with a pink ribbon tied around the waist. She pranced back and forth near her mother, sometimes weaving between her mother and brothers, making a game of it. I had only seen her one time before, a little while back.

Grayson had been in the diner at his usual booth, with his papers and books spread across the table. He had been unusually serious that afternoon. I think it wasn't long after his arrest at the protest for the homeless. But his eyes lit up when his wife and daughter came into the diner. His wife sat across from him, but his daughter climbed right up on his lap. She threw her arms around him and gave him a kiss on his cheek.

"Hi, pumpkin," he said. "What are you up to?"

"Mommy and I went to get our nails done," she said as she held out both hands so he could see the bright pink on her nails.

"Well, that's just about the prettiest thing I've ever seen," he said. "Is that a new ring, too?"

She beamed and nodded her head in an exaggerated manner. I brought them some milkshakes and she squealed with excitement. Grayson seemed as happy as I had ever seen him. As I watched him—watched them—a heaviness returned that I hadn't felt since I had gone to his church. I tried to busy myself with other tables and other tasks, but no matter how hard I tried, my eyes kept being drawn to that little girl. After she and her mother left, I went to clear the dishes from the table.

"Your daughter is beautiful," I said.

He smiled. "She takes after her mother."

"She has your eyes, though," I said. His cheeks flushed red and then I felt my own cheeks flush. "I didn't mean…"

"It's okay, Ramie. I know what you meant." I wanted him to look away, to get back to his books and papers, but he kept staring at me. "Are you all right? You look distressed."

That's all he had to say for the rush of tears to come. I tried to turn but he stopped me.

"What is it?" he said. His voice held all of the concern I had come to expect from him.

I looked over and saw the only other customers get up from their table. They were puzzled, and uncomfortable, when they saw the tears lining my cheeks, but they waved as they walked out the door. As soon as they left, I sat down across from Grayson and tried to gather myself. He closed his books and waited patiently, letting me come to whatever I wanted to say in my own time.

"I've never told anyone this," I finally said, my eyes not leaving their focus on the table in front of me. "I had a little girl, but she died. I was only fifteen when I got pregnant. Like so many girls at that age, I thought I was in love and I thought he loved me. Of course as soon as he found out I was pregnant, he wanted nothing more to do with me. I cried myself to sleep for a month until Daddy told me that I needed to get myself together because I was going to be responsible for another human life soon.

"Daddy tried to take care of me because I was pretty sick. What I didn't know at the time was that he was also sick. Maybe he didn't know it either, but I think he did and was just trying to protect me. Anyway, Annaleigh was born and she was beautiful. She had a headful of black hair just like my daddy. He smiled so big when he saw her, like he himself had been reborn. But within a few days after Annaleigh came home, he got very sick. The day before he died, he told me that even though I hadn't had a good role model, he knew I was going to be a good mommy. I saw the sadness in his eyes when he said it. Thinking of Mommy hurt us both.

"After he died, I tried my best to take care of Annaleigh. But I was so tired because I was doing it on my own, with nobody to help me. One morning I woke up late and realized that she hadn't cried all night. When I checked on her, she was blue and cold to the touch. Even when they took her away and told me that it sometimes happens to babies that young and that it can't be explained, I still felt guilty. I was worse than my own mother. But I loved Annaleigh with all my heart.

"Maybe that was the problem. Everyone I ever loved was taken from me. Do you think God is punishing me for something I've done? I mean, sometimes I think he is." I finally lifted my eyes to meet his. I desperately searched for comfort there.

He took my hand. "No, Ramie, not at all. God doesn't work that way. Not the God I know. In fact, I'm pretty sure that God has grieved with you through all that you have lost. Unfortunately this is a fallen and broken world, and bad things happen, even to good people."

It had to be a broken world for someone like Grayson to be taken. Without meaning to, I caught a glimpse of his face just behind one of his sons. I felt sick to my stomach.

"Are you all right?" the woman behind me in line asked. "You look pale."

"Yes," I said, a bit embarrassed. "I think I just need to sit for a few minutes." I smiled weakly at her and then found a seat near the back of the room and rested my head on the back of the chair in front of me.

"Hi," I heard a tiny voice say. I looked up and it was Grayson's little girl.

"Hi," I said back. "What's your name?"

"Hannah," she said as she fidgeted with her dress, lifting the skirt up from the hem to reveal her white tights. My heart ached imagining this is what my Annaleigh might have been like.

"You're so pretty, Miss Hannah. I love your dress and those pretty patent leather shoes." She giggled, pleased with the compliment.

"I knew your daddy," I said.

"Everyone knew my daddy," she said matter-of-factly.

"Yes. That's because he was a nice person," I said. "He helped me so many times, like I'm sure he helped everybody." I looked at her and it was like looking at him. "You know, Hannah, your daddy is in heaven, up there in the sky like a star—and the Bible says that God knows every star and calls them each by name. I bet if you look up there tonight you'll be able to see your daddy shining down on you." She smiled, showing her missing front teeth, and then she flounced back to her mother, who lifted her up and hugged her tight. I was surprised by the comfort that image brought to me. In the midst of sorrow there was love.

I didn't need to go through the line. I didn't even need to say a final good-bye. Grayson taught me that love survives and that was enough. When I got home, I picked up Daddy's guitar and began to mindlessly strum. And then the chords began to take on a familiar sound, and the words formed in my mind.

Amazing Grace, How sweet the sound
That saved a wretch like me

Daddy didn't like most religious music, but there was something about that song that always spoke comfort to him. He said that maybe it was because he liked the thought that grace could lead us home. For me, home had been hard to find and certainly hard to keep. The truth was that I had been so lost I was certain I'd never find my way home, even though I'd been searching for so long. But as I strummed the familiar chords, I heard Grayson's voice.

"Let go, Ramie. You were lost, but now you're found. Grace has led you home."

HANNAH

My daddy is that star in the sky.

NATALIE

I WAS SUPPOSED TO say goodbye today. That's what funerals are for, isn't it? But how is that possible when everything feels so raw, so unfinished? We were supposed to have a lifetime together. That's what you promised, Grayse. How could *you* break that promise?

Do you know what Hannah said to me this morning? She said, "Don't be sad, Mommy. Daddy's in the sky. I saw him last night and I made a wish." Where does she get these things? She's only six, I know, but sometimes she's such an old soul. Maybe that's because she wasn't a child of our youth, like Tyler and Blake.

She was good as gold today. I hope you saw that. She sat beside me and didn't squirm much, even though she wanted to chase the butterflies skimming the flowers just outside the green awning. They were beautiful specks of color gliding through the nothingness, being what they were created to be and doing what they were created to do. Did they hear the words, or did the words float on by them, through the nothingness into nothingness?

Maybe instead they heard the buzzing of the bees competing for the delicate pollen. Or maybe the rustle of cellophane as tissues moved from hand to hand. Do you know what tears sound like? They are muted sniffs. They come from behind you like a chorus, so quiet at first that you aren't aware of the sound. The chorus builds—new voices join in to harmonize until you can hear nothing else. Mourning rising to a crescendo and then falling to silent grief. Words drift by until you can snatch only one or two at a time—counterpoint. Ashes to ashes...we commend our brother... to almighty God...dust to dust.

Do you remember the time at the beach, back when Tyler was little and I was pregnant with Blake? We built a sandcastle together. It was the biggest one on the beach and we all stood back and admired it. Even strangers came by and took pictures. Tyler loved it, but he couldn't wait to knock it down. I told him no because it had taken so much effort to build. But you persuaded me to let him. "For a two-year-old, the tearing down can be more fun than the building up," you said with your bright eyes and boyish smile. "Very little in this life is permanent, particularly sand castles," you called back through the salty breeze as you and Tyler raced to begin the demolition. While I witnessed you and your son level the sandcastle, the innocent joy on your faces filled my heart. At that moment I knew why I had always loved you.

At sunset we walked side by side just above the breaking water's edge. Tyler straddled your neck and his brown legs dangled across your shoulders. Our feet sank in the wet sand and stamped oversize footprints that trailed behind us. I gazed over my shoulder to see the path we had walked, but it was there only a moment before the evening tide washed over our footprints. The waves receded smoothing the sand, erasing them—as if they were never there. Back then you and I marveled how nature had a way of restoring itself, of cropping us from the picture. Back then it was comforting to think that nature could erase our presence. But it brings no comfort now. Not today, knowing your footprints are gone forever.

HANK

THE FIRST TIME I ever saw the reverend he was sitting in the shade of the old florist shop leaning against the brick wall with his head resting on his knees. I'd seen that posture with other people—it's a sure sign that the last drop of hope has finally evaporated. I thought about walking on by when I saw him. Sometimes a man just needs to be alone with his misery. But something made me stop. It wasn't his dirty jeans or ripped T-shirt or even the sneakers about to come apart at the seams. Most of the people I hung around with looked like some variation of that. No, thinking back on it now, I think it was because he looked out of place—an anachronism, a blip of the future in this tradition-laden town. Whatever it was, it drew me to him like a magnet.

"How long have you been on the streets?" I said when I got close. He looked up at me, raising his arms to shade his eyes. He was younger than I expected, but then again, homelessness doesn't understand age.

"On the streets?" He seemed puzzled, and then looked down at his clothes. "Oh. Not long. How about you?"

"A few years."

"That long, huh? That doesn't give much hope." He tried to smile. "I'm sure it's been difficult." He motioned for me to sit next to him and I did.

"You learn to adapt," I said. "Every now and then I stay a couple of nights at a shelter or sleep on someone's couch, especially when it gets too cold. I can't stand the cold."

"Do you ever go to any of the churches for help. Surely they help."

"A few do."

"Have you ever been to that one?" He pointed to the church across the empty parking lot. "I thought about going there for help. I mean their name is New Hope."

"Don't count on any kind of hope from them."

"Really? What makes you say that?"

"Let's just say that they don't have any fucking sympathy for people in our situation. Oh, they'll give you a couple of cans of food, but don't let them catch you hanging around too long because you'll get chased off. They've even called the cops a couple of times on one of my buddies because he was sitting all afternoon in the doorway of that building over there. He was just sitting in the fucking doorway minding his own business."

"That sure doesn't seem very Christian of them."

"I think they see us as modern-day lepers. You know, unclean. I guess they haven't gotten to the 'love your neighbor' and 'come to me, you weary and heavy laden' part." He smiled at me. "What's so funny?" I said.

"I was just thinking— I'm sorry, I didn't catch your name."

"Hank. Hank Connelly."

"I'm Grayson Armstrong." We shook hands. "I was just thinking, Hank, that you'd make a good preacher."

"Now that is funny. It would be a cold day in hell if I was ever to set foot in a church, let alone get up in front of one."

He laughed. "Sounds like—" He stopped when a man in old clothes and holding a paint brush came out of the side door of the church.

"Pastor Armstrong, all the guys are here now," he hollered.

"Pastor?" I said as I jump to my feet. "What the—"

He jumped to his feet as well, putting one hand on my arm and the other up to signal he wanted me to stay put. "Thanks, Jason," he called to the man. "You all can go ahead and get started. I'll be there when I get finished." The man waved and went back inside the church. The reverend turned to me, his face scrunched up. He could see the question still lingering on mine. "Yes, I'm the new pastor at the church. I'm sorry for the deception," he said.

"You should be, Reverend. I would never have said those things if I'd known—"

"That's why I didn't say anything. And, please, it's just Grayson.

I hate fancy titles. I'm having enough trouble breaking the church people of that." He smiled and I felt at ease again. "Frankly, I needed some clarity and I didn't think I'd get an authentic perspective if you knew who I was."

"You're probably right."

"Let me buy you something to eat, as a way of making it up to you."

I should have said no, but I was damn hungry. We walked to the diner across the street. I was a bit uneasy because I'd been chased away from their dumpsters several times, so I didn't know what they'd think with me coming in there.

It was busy, which always makes me anxious. I don't like crowds. "Be right with you," the waitress said as she whizzed by us with a plate of food. "No hurry," the reverend called back to her in his friendliest voice. He smiled at me and I just shrugged my shoulders. After a couple of minutes of us standing there like a couple of idiots, she finally came and took us to a booth in the back corner, where I'm sure we couldn't be seen. She shoved menus at us and walked away without saying anything, like I was already invisible.

"Sorry about your wait," she said when she finally came back. "You ready to order?"

"We were ready ten minutes ago," I snapped.

"It's okay," the reverend said. "We're not in any hurry, are we, Hank?"

"No, I guess not."

He smiled and looked up at the waitress, which made her soften toward us—at least toward him. When she brought our burgers a little later, she was practically glowing. "You let me know if you all need anything else," she chirped as she turned to go. It took me by surprise how he had managed such a transformation in her mood, but the truth was that same undeniable charm had its own effect on me, because I found myself lost in his throaty laughter as I shared one story after another of my antics during college—before I was drafted in my sophomore year. How long it had been since I had laughed like that, since I had felt a real kinship with someone. I kept looking at this man I had just met and wondered how he could so quickly scale the wall I'd built around me and reach in to let loose fragments of my life I'd locked away for safekeeping. It scared me. He had found the pieces that made him laugh but I don't think he could handle the wreckage that lay at the core of my being. I had to protect that—protect him from the ugliness of it.

After we finished eating, we walked back. I wondered what he was going to say when he got back to the church after being gone so long. He had clearly abandoned his work there so that he could feed me.

"You made my day, Hank," he said as he shook my hand. "I'm glad you chose to check on me when you saw me sitting there."

"So what *were* you doing over there?"

"I was praying for direction." He smiled warmly. "And then you showed up."

I didn't understand his meaning but I nodded as if I did.

NATALIE

TIME HAS STOPPED. THE cloud outside my bedroom window was rising and billowing into the blue sky like a plume of smoke. It isn't rising anymore. It isn't moving—no movement at all. It's frozen in time.

Everything is past tense now. Time has stopped. There is no future tense—not even a present tense. There is no now.

"Blessed are the dead who die in the Lord. They rest from their labors, and their works follow them."

YOUR FOOTPRRINTS HAVE BEEN all over my life Grayse. I cannot bear the thought of you being erased from my world. I see you in the faces and the spirits of our children. I see you in Effie and Fred and the many other people you changed by your presence in their lives. I see you in Hank. I want to hate Hank for taking you away but I hear your words and I know I will—someday—find comfort. *Forgiveness is the most humbling and challenging act of spiritual obedience.*

ACKNOWLEDGMENTS

WRITING A NOVEL OFTEN requires a great deal of solitude, but the completed book would never come about if not for the support and encouragement of others. For that reason, I wish to thank Shadelandhouse Modern Press, Virginia Underwood, and Stephanie Underwood for believing in this book, for the thoughtful editing, and for guiding me through the publication process.

Throughout the writing process, I sought strength and inspiration through the written word of great authors like Lee Smith, Silas House, and Denise Giardina, among others. I was encouraged by friends and family as they listened to early drafts. To Kelli Brown, Jeani Lloyd, and Sheila Virgin, your friendship means so much to me. To my sons, Nathan and Adam, and my daughter-in-law, Jeretta, I am grateful for your love and support. To pastors like Tiger Pennington, Angie Messinger, and Lynn Buckles, I am humbled by your godly examples.

Finally, to my husband, Glenn, I am fortunate that you are always by my side. You have never hesitated to support my dreams, to be a good sounding board when I need one, and to hold me tight when life sometimes hits a bump. This book would have never happened without you.

ABOUT THE AUTHOR

Sherry Robinson, an American fiction writer, is currently Vice Provost and Professor of English at Eastern Kentucky University, Richmond, Kentucky. She received a PhD in English from the University of Kentucky and an MA in English from Eastern Kentucky University. She taught American Literature before moving into administrative roles. Robinson is the author of two novels, *Blessed* and *My Secrets Cry Aloud.*

PRAISE FOR *MY SECRETS CRY ALOUD*

SHERRY ROBINSON has the ability to go right to the heart of things: a family, a personality...She does not gloss over or neglect the real complexity of life.—LEE SMITH, author of Dimestore

[A] beautifully written novel filled with wisdom and keen insights in a calm, clear voice, and a book that you will carry with you long after you've finished.—SILAS HOUSE, author of Southernmost